Season of Secrets

SALLY NICHOLLS

Season
of Secrets

ARTHUR A. LEVINE BOOKS
An imprint of Scholastic Inc.

Text copyright © 2009 by Sally Nicholls • All rights reserved. Published by Arthur A. Levine Books, an imprint of Scholastic Inc., *Publishers since 1920*, by arrangement with Scholastic Ltd., London, England. SCHOLASTIC, the LANTERN LOGO, and associated logos are trademarks and/or registered trademarks of Scholastic Inc. No part of this publication may be reproduced, stored in a retrieval system, or transmitted in any form or by any means, electronic, mechanical, photocopying, recording, or otherwise, without written permission of the publisher. For information regarding permission, write to Scholastic Inc., Attention: Permissions Department, 557 Broadway, New York, NY 10012. Library of Congress Cataloging-in-Publication Data Nicholls, Sally, 1983– Season of secrets / Sally Nicholls. — 1st American ed. p. cm. Summary: Sent by their father to live in the country with their grandparents after the sudden death of their mother, Molly's older sister Hannah expresses her grief in a raging rebellion while imaginative Molly finds herself increasingly distracted by visions, that seemingly only she can see, of a strange hunt in the nearby forest. ISBN 978-0-545-21825-2 (hardcover : alk. paper) [1. Grief — Fiction. 2. Sisters — Fiction. 3. Family problems — Fiction. 4. Green Man (Tale) — Fiction. 5. England — Fiction.] I. Title. PZ7.N524Se 2011 [Fic] — dc22 2010017070 • 10 9 8 7 6 5 4 3 2 1   11 12 13 14 15
• Printed in the U.S.A.   23 • First American edition, January 2011

To my family,
For sticking around.

Contents

I'm Molly. Molly Alice Brooke on school registers. If you're a friend of mine, or someone in my family maybe, then I'm Moll too. If you're an adult in my family, which right now is complicated, then I'm love, or Molly-love, or curly-mop, or sweetheart. At my old school I was molly-mop. At Christmas I was an angel and a hotel keeper.

Names are important. Everyone has one, except really tiny babies maybe, or stray dogs, or people who've forgotten who they are. And even stray dogs and people with amnesia have names. They've just forgotten them.

And then there's the hunted man. He didn't have any name at all.

1

The Roman Road

It's raining when we come up the hill from school today. A sudden, heavy flash of rainstorm; here then gone. Hannah sticks her school bag over her head and stamps through the puddles.

"Back *home* we never had to walk in the rain. Back *home* someone would've picked us up. In a *car.*"

"They wouldn't have just driven down a street to get us," I say. Hannah's always so sure she's right. Talking to her leaves me full of half-finished arguments, dangling fights I know I should have won. If Mum and Dad were here, they wouldn't drive down a poksey hill just to save us getting wet. We only got picked up at home because we went to some stupid school miles across town. "We had to wait at after-school club till someone finished work. And then we had to do shopping. And if it was gymnastics or piano we had to have tea in the car. In a *box.* And —"

"At least *someone* came," says Hannah. "Someone *cared.*"

Someone is Mum.

"Grandpa cares," I say, but I don't think she hears me. Hannah is one and a half years older than me, yet she takes up about one and a half million times more space.

The trees in the gardens up the hill rustle, as if they're talking about us. But trees don't talk. I look at them over my shoulder, all raindropped and rain-drooped, and hurry after Hannah.

She's pushing open the door to Grandpa's shop. She stands inside and shakes herself, drops of water smattering the bread and the biscuits, leaving dark spatters on the newspapers in their rack.

"I *hate* this place!" she says. Loudly.

I come in small behind her. I don't hate this place. Grandpa and Grandma's shop. It's poky and dark and higgledy-piggledy. It sells a mess of things I've never seen in normal shops, like Eccles cakes and Ordnance Survey maps and homemade jam, next to ordinary boringables like Coco Pops and Fairy Liquid. There's a misty fridge with milk bottles with JONES and ENTLY written across them in felt tip, in case people go home with the wrong bottle. You can order more exotic things — mangoes or ricotta cheese — if you don't mind waiting for the van, though most people don't, they just go to Tesco's. In one corner, there's a metal grille where the post office used to be and in another are baskets of earthy potatoes and onions. It has a friendly, muddly smell all its own: newspaper and bleach and earth.

Grandma's leaning against the counter, writing in a big accounts book. She looks up when we come in and her face tightens.

"Hannah Brooke," she says. "Have a bit of sense now! Stop dripping all over the floor. Go on," she says, when Hannah doesn't move. "Get upstairs and into something dry."

Hannah kicks the shelf.

"No!" she shouts, and then her face screws up like she's going to cry. "I want to go home," she says instead, ridiculously.

Grandma doesn't fight her, like Mum would have done, but you can tell she's angry. She comes out from behind the till, presses her hand on Hannah's shoulder, and pushes her through the door into the kitchen, where Grandpa's mashing the tea and whistling.

"Upstairs," she tells Grandpa. "Clean clothes. Now." And she stalks back into the shop.

Hannah's face twists. It's pink and white with cold, and streaked with blue dye where her bag's run in the rain. You can see the fight boiling up inside her.

"*Go and die in a field!*" she screams at the door and Grandma's back. Then she runs out of the room, up the stairs.

Me and Grandpa are left in the kitchen. Grandpa rubs at his face, just the way my dad does. He breathes in this big breath — I can see his stomach rising, under the faded checked cloth of his shirt. It's gone a nasty yellow around his neck and against the cuffs. My dad's shirts are always stiff and clean and white; you button him up all the way to his throat and there he is, locked up safe and going nowhere. But Grandpa Lived Through A War, so he wears things till they fall apart.

"All right, love?" he says now, and I nod. "*You* don't want me to die in a field, do you?" he says, and I shake my head.

"You shouldn't listen to Hannah," I tell him. "She's always like that. Dad should have put her in an orphanage or something, instead of sending her here. She would have liked that, I expect," I add, virtuous, "since she doesn't want to live here."

Grandpa comes over and pats my shoulder. "Now, now," he says, in an absent sort of way. "No one's going to any orphanage."

But why not? If Dad could send us here, he could send us anywhere.

I go through the back door of the shop, into the hall, and up the narrow stairs. The shop is part of Grandma and Grandpa's house, so all of their rooms are muddled: The kitchen is downstairs, next to the storeroom, but the living room is upstairs. At night, when I lie in bed, the light from the television flickers against the landing wall, and studio laughter plays across my dreams. Everything is darker here, and older. Nothing matches, so you'll have our old settee from Newcastle next to a high-backed red chair with feet like a lion. There's a dark wood bookcase with glass doors, where Delia Smith and Dick Francis sit beside ancient cloth-bound books with gold and silver printed up the spine.

The room I have here was Auntie Meg's when she was my age. It's got horrible yellow wallpaper and a grown-up picture of a tree, and a yellowy sink in the corner that doesn't work. Some of my things are here — my old bear, Humphrey, my best books, my art things. But nearly all of my stuff is still at home, because we're not staying here forever, just until Dad gets things Sorted Out.

Whenever that is.

I take dry clothes out of the wardrobe — blue jeans and my soft yellow sweater — but I don't put them on. I wrap my arms around them and stand by the window looking out over the garden. The rain is rat-a-tat-tat-ing on the roof and streaming down the windows. The trees are roaring with the wind in them, more like they're fighting now than talking.

"Listen!" Mum would say, if she was here. "There's a night with a devil in it."

It wouldn't be a bad thing — the devil in the night — but something exciting. Mum loved thunder-and-rain-storms. If she were here now, like if we were staying with Grandpa and Grandma because it was a holiday maybe, we'd all go out and jump in the puddles. Even Hannah would, probably.

It's not dark yet, but you can tell that tonight isn't going to be fun. The sky is full of anger and the trees are raging like they want to kill someone. Standing here alone by the window, I almost believe in a devil in the rain.

Inside, the house is full of fighting too. I can hear Hannah next door, crying. I can hear Grandma down-stairs, her voice high and angry, and Grandpa, murmuring at her.

I put on my dry clothes and climb into bed, pulling the funny old-fashioned quilt-and-blanket over my head. I get my book out and read, trying not to listen to the loneliness of being alone in a house full of noise. I'm reading *Three Cheers, Secret Seven*, which is Secret Seven book eight, so when I'm done I'll only need to read seven more and I'll have read all the Famous Five and Secret Seven books there are.

Outside, the rain falls quieter now.

It's getting dark.

"Molly? Are you there?"

Hannah is standing in the doorway, still in her wet clothes. There are two wet patches on her shoulders where the water's run off her hair and onto her sweater.

"Come on," she says. "Quick — before they find us."

"What are we doing?"

"*Shhh.*" She clutches my arm and pulls me toward the edge of the bed. "We're going home. We're running away."

This is so surprising that for a moment I can only blink at her. This is way more my sort of thing than Hannah's. I've read loads of books about people running away. Hannah only reads *Girl Talk* and *Top of the Pops Magazine.* She'll have no idea what to do.

"Hey," I say. "Ha*nnaah.* Stop *pulling.* We need to pack. Sleeping bags — and food — and a knife — and toothpaste —"

"Where d'you think we're going?" says Hannah. "The Arctic? We don't need any of that stuff. We'll just walk to Hexham and get the train."

There's a big map of Northumberland up on the landing. Hannah and I count off the miles to Hexham on the old Roman road.

"Seven — eight — nine — ten. Ten miles! We can walk that. Come on!"

She drags me downstairs. I want to argue, but I don't want Grandma to hear. Tonight isn't a night to be running away. It's dark and furious outside.

"We can't walk ten miles," I say. "Ha*nnaah*. That'll take ages. It's *miles*. Can't we go in the morning?"

"We're going *now*," says Hannah. She tugs on my arm and I nearly fall.

"What about Grandpa? What'll he do when he finds we've gone?"

"Who cares?" says Hannah. She lets go of my sleeve and starts rummaging through the coats on the rack. I can hear the radio playing next door in the kitchen, and the hiss of fat from Grandpa frying sausages.

"Hannah?"

"What?"

"What about Dad?"

Hannah stops, one arm half into her jacket.

"What *about* Dad?"

"Won't he just send us back here?"

There's a silence. I look up. Hannah's standing perfectly still, her jacket still dangling from one arm.

"I don't care," she says, "what Dad does. And I don't care what he says. I'm not staying here any longer." And she pulls open the door, wet wind blowing into the porch, and runs into the night.

I hesitate for a moment. Then I run out after her.

Once outside, the air is wet and cold, and full of the smell and icy spat of rain. The wind blows the hood of my sweater up against the back of my head. My coat's still hanging on the peg, and behind me the door slams shut. We're locked outside.

"Hannah!" I shout. "Hannah! Wait for me!"

Someone answers, but I can't tell from where. To my left, the lane curls out across the fields and up onto the moor. To my right, it slopes down the hill into the village, curving round across the village green and over the humpback bridge, past the church and the school and the little pub with the swinging FULL MOON sign with the picture of the man in the moon. Is it up the lane or through the village to get to Hexham? Hannah would know, but I don't. I go up, out of the village.

It's dark. Much darker than it ever gets at home. No streetlights. No house lights. I have to feel for every step, arms outstretched in case I fall; I can hardly see where I'm going. I splash straight into a puddle.

"Ha*nnaah*!"

I duck my head, screw up my eyes against the rain, and stump up the lane. The wind rushes through the trees, sending the rain back to blow in my face. I stumble and almost fall. It's the devil in the night — the devil in the storm. It's in the trees. I stop walking. I don't want to go to Hexham on my own. I don't even know how to get there. In fact, the farther I go, the more certain I am that Hannah's gone the other way.

Or maybe she's gone back to Grandpa's and left me here alone.

It's so pitchy-black and rainy, it's hard to tell how far I've gone. The moon's risen, a silver thumbnail shining through dark, rushing clouds. The lane has narrowed and the trees on the steep banks are closer. They send long, dark branch-fingers looming and roaring over my head.

"I'm not afraid," I say out loud.

Because now I can hear something coming. Someone. Feet. Feet running toward me. My heart jumps. Who would be out on a wild night like this? Alone, without a light? It's the devil — I know it is. I turn and stumble-run up the bank, slipping and almost falling in the mud. I'm not going to make it. I'm going to be in the lane when he comes. My breath comes out in raggedy gasps and I think I'm almost crying. There is something so sinister about the running footsteps — dark noises alone in a black night — that stops my heart. But then there I am, almost in the hedgerow. I grab on to the branch of a hawthorn tree, thorns catching at my sweater and my fingers, and hold my breath.

And here he is. A dark shape, bent and running. It's a

man, low and strong. He's so close I can hear his breath catch in his throat.

And then he's past, off down the road to the village. But now I can hear other noises — a horn, then another horn, and another. Coming closer. Horses. Dogs, barking. *Baying*. That's what dogs do, in hunts, when they smell their prey.

The running man has heard them. He looks back. His face is white in the darkness and wet with rain. He isn't wearing shoes, or a shirt. I can see his chest, rising and falling. I can feel how frightened he is. Who is he? Who's chasing him?

And then the dogs are here.

They charge round the corner and pour onto him. They're huge, more like wolves than dogs. He falls, lifting his arms to cover his face. And now the huntsmen are here, black shapes on tall horses. The lead huntsman stops and raises his head, and I have to clench my lips to stop myself screaming. He's got *horns* growing out of his hair, great tall antlers rising up out of the sides of his head. I press myself deep into the hawthorn tree until twigs dig into my back and thorns tear at my sweater. *Don't see me. Don't see me. Don't see me.*

The lead huntsman sits tall on his tall horse. He raises a black hunting horn to his lips and blows, a long clear note.

I squeeze my eyes shut tight.

And . . .

. . . they're gone.

I don't move. I keep my eyes shut. I can still smell the horses and the huntsman, but the noises have gone. All I can hear is my heart and the quick, snuffly sound of my breath going in-and-out-and-in-and-out. And the rain. They must still be there, they must, they must —

There's a noise. A small one, something shifting, pebbles moving. I open my eyes. The lane is empty. The horses — the man — the dogs — they've gone. But something's still there, scrabbling in the lane.

Hawthorn trees aren't made to be held on to. They have too many prickles and not enough big branches. I shift and slip and slide into the lane, mud all down my legs and back. I struggle and fall forward. Onto something — some*one* warm.

I scream. I scream and scream and hands come up and hold my shoulders, warm, living hands.

"Hush. Shhh. Shhh." The voice is low and strong against the rain. I scramble back, terrified, and the hands let go. "No one's going to hurt you. Shhh."

It's not the hunter. It's the other one. The hunted man.

All of a sudden, I start to cry, gaspy, shuddery sobs. The hunted man sits back and watches me. I can see in the darkness that he's young, that his face is wet with sweat and rain, that his hair curls.

"There," he says, in his low voice. "Nobody's hurt. Nobody's hurting you."

"You're hurt," I say.

He is. His legs are all torn up by the wolf-dogs. Dark blood oozes out and over the ragged cloth of his trousers, rain and cloth and blood. Sobs shudder up inside me again and I look quickly away.

"Nobody's hurt," he says again. He looks at me. "Are you far from home?" I shake my head, and "Go home," he says. "You shouldn't be out at night. Didn't your mother tell you that?"

"My mother's dead," I say, and I start crying again.

There's a noise in the lane, bushes rustling. I tense, squeezing my stomach to keep the tears inside. The man grips my arm and lifts his nose like an animal, sniffing danger.

There's a rustle from the bushes and a bird rises; a crow, I think, wings flapping madly and then gone. The man's grip on my arm relaxes and I hiccup, aware suddenly of how stupid I must look, snot and tears dripping down my face, covered in mud.

The hunted man leans forward. "Go home," he says again, more urgently. "Do you want the wild hunt to find you?" But I'm frightened again and don't answer.

He grips my arm. "Go well," he says. "Go safely. But go now."

There are only the two of us in the darkness, only the two of us in the whole world. I don't want to leave him, but I don't want to stay here either. I stumble back to my feet and down the lane, to home.

2

Nowhere Man

I've not gone far when I see a light, and hear a voice calling.

"Molly! Molly!"

"Grandma!" I run straight into her.

"Molly!" She holds me to her, then pulls me away and shakes me; not hard, but enough to shock me. "What did you want to run off like that for? Haven't we all got enough to worry about?"

"I didn't —" I say, and I start crying all over again. Grandma puts her arm round me.

"Hey, shush. *Shush*. None of that. Grandma's got you."

But I remember.

"Grandma! There's a man."

She pulls back.

"A man?"

"He's hurt." I know exactly where he is, by the hawthorn tree. I point. "Look."

Grandma shines her torch where I'm pointing. There's nothing there but lane.

"You aren't telling stories again, are you, Moll?"

"No! Look! I'll show you!"

I pull her closer.

"Hey now, Moll, slow down. Easy does it. Where was he?"

"Here!" I grab her hand and swing the torch around. There's the hawthorn tree, and the muddy streak where I fell down the bank, but no man. I run forward trying to see where he's gone.

"Hey!" I call. "Where are you?"

"Moll," says Grandma. "*Molly!* Come back here. Come on. Tell me what's going on."

I run back.

"There was a man, a weird man, without shoes or a shirt or anything, running down the lane, and then this hunt came out of nowhere, a proper hunt, with dogs — wolves, really — and a man with horns growing out of his head and everything. And the wolves got him, and they would have got me, only I was hiding. And then they vanished, all the hunt and everyone, except him, and he talked to me and he told me to go well and go safely and go now, so I did and then —"

"And then he vanished," says Grandma. "Or turned into a teapot?"

"Yes," I say. "I mean, no. He just vanished. But he was here! Look!"

I grab her torch hand again and point it on the patch of lane where he was lying.

"What am I looking at?" grumbles Grandma.

"Here!" I say. "No — here — no, wait — it's here somewhere, I know it is." I pull her closer. "There! Look, it's blood! That's where he was lying!"

It's hard, in the darkness, to tell where the rain and the mud and the bloodstains begin and end. Grandma peers shortsightedly downward.

"Could be," she says at last. "Could be a fox has been out, killing rabbits. Let's go home now, Moll. I'm old and I'm wet through."

"But the man," I say. "He's hurt!"

"If he's not here now," says Grandma, "he can't be too badly hurt. If he's got any sense he'll have gone home too. In any case, I think we should go home and tell Grandpa and Hannah that we've found you."

So Hannah did go back. I should have known she wouldn't really run away. I feel cheated, suddenly, of my adventure — and my moment as the sensible one. Now I'm the little one, doing the wrong thing again.

Grandma holds out her hand and I take it.

"You think I'm making it up, don't you?" I say. I *did*

used to make up stories, when I was little, but I don't anymore.

"Me?" says Grandma. "I think I've got much more important things to worry about."

Which doesn't exactly mean that she believes me.

3

Night Thoughts

Grandpa's coming up the hill when we get back.

"Molly-love —" he says. "What happened? Are —"

"She's fine," says Grandma, before I can answer. "She could do with a bath, though — look at her."

Grandpa takes me up to the bathroom without saying anything else. He runs the bath. Afterward he puts me to bed in my narrow little bedroom, with a plate of cold sausages and hard yellow potatoes. He sits on my bed and waits until I'm done. The curtains have been drawn against the night, but I don't look out. I don't like to think about what might still be out there.

"We'll get your things fixed soon," says Grandpa. "Bring some of your pictures from home and put them up, eh?"

"Mmm," I say. Dad promised we were only here for a visit. Putting pictures up is a bit too much like staying for good.

"Dad's coming on Saturday," Grandpa says. "That'll be nice, won't it?"

"Yes."

"Good." He pats my hand, awkwardly. "You would tell me if something was bothering you, wouldn't you, Molly-love? Hannah or school or . . . or anything?"

"Mmm," I say again. I squirm down further into the bed. Grandpa sighs.

"All right." He creaks up and kisses my forehead. "Sleep tight, sweetheart."

After he's gone, I lie on my back and stare at the ceiling. Above my head, the rain is pattering on the roof. I remember the hunted man, his voice in the darkness saying, "Nobody's hurt. Nobody's hurting you." I wonder where he is now. I wonder if he's found somewhere dry to sleep. I wonder if the hunt has found him.

I remember his hands, holding me, how gentle they were. I remember the kindness in his voice, saying, "Shhh. No one's going to hurt you. Shhh."

4
The World According to Books

There's only one thing I like about this bedroom and that's the windowsill. It's big and deep, and if you sit on it with a book and pull the curtains closed behind you, you can pretend you're in a secret room and no one in the world can find you.

I've always been a bookworm, and I've been reading even more since we came here and stopped having drama classes and gymnastics and piano lessons all the time. There's a bookcase in the hall that is full of Dad's and Auntie Meg's books from when they were kids. Really old hardback ones like *Peter Pan* and *Swallows and Amazons* and books about Girl Guides. I know most of them already, because I always read them when we come on visits.

I would like to live in a book. The world works better in books. If you go on picnics, the sun shines. If something gets stolen, you can solve the crime just by thinking hard. If someone's dying, calling 999 will save them. It's always obvious who's good and who's bad, and kids can camp out on moors or go to the North Pole or be world-famous detectives aged only ten.

Everything is simpler in books. In books, lost fathers always come back from the dead and bullies always get beaten. The sun always shines on your birthday and things always work out right in the end.

5

A Face Like That

"You made him up," says Hannah.

We're coming down the hill to school.

"You always say that," I say. "Why do you always say that? He was real. He was *there*."

"It's always made up," says Hannah. "The stuff you say you've seen. Either that or you've gone crazy." She looks at me thoughtfully. "Do you hear voices? Do they tell you to do things? *Kill Grandma, Molly. Kiill heeeerrr. . . .*"

"Shove off." I hunch my bag on my shoulders. "If it wasn't for you, I'd never have been there. What did you have to go back to Grandpa's and leave me there for, anyway?"

"We couldn't have really got all the way home, you know," says Hannah, in her older-sister voice, like it was all my idea in the first place, and she runs off down the hill before I can answer.

I follow after.

How do you know if something's real? Shadows on the wall, noises in the night, scurrying shapes that might be mice or little men or merely imaginings. The man last night *felt* real. But then so do dreams. Are dreams real?

"Come on!" shouts Hannah, over her shoulder.

Our school here is tiny — a square stone building with a postage stamp of yard and a scrubby playing field across the road. There's only one classroom and one round table that everyone sits round. There's one class and eight people in it.

We're late. The others are inside. Sascha — who's six — is standing by the empty hamster cage, crying.

"I only wanted to stroke him!"

Everyone else is watching Josh and Matthew, who are flat on their bellies under the Nature Table, shouting.

"I can see him!"

"Don't let him get away!"

Josh and Matthew are like Hannah. They take up a lot of space. They're brothers. They hang around with Alexander, who's leaning over the table, also shouting.

"No — not like that! Try and trap him —"

Alexander's sort of plump. His blue school sweater is twisted up one shoulder and it's already got orange juice spilled down it. His parents both work for the University of Northumbria. He's the sort of boy who knows far more about Romans than is good for anybody.

"No, look —"

Josh and Matthew ignore him. Only Oliver, who is four and the smallest person in the school, turns and stares at him, round pink face, brown eyes, and a wet red mouth chewing on his sweater cuff.

That leaves Emily. Emily isn't chasing hamsters. Emily has fair hair and blue eyes and sparkly silver shoes. Emily's by the water tray, looking out the window.

Outside, the sky is gray.

It's going to rain again.

"All right!" Mrs. Angus has come in from the kitchen. "Joshua Haltwhistle, get out from under there *right now*! Now!"

"I've got him!" Josh comes slithering out, hamster cupped in his hand, hair speckled with bits of Nature Table mushroom.

"And just what did you think you were doing?" Mrs. Angus starts into Josh, who's indignant.

"We were helping! Sascha let the hamster out!"

Mrs. Angus ignores him. Mrs. Angus is the teaching assistant, but very fierce.

Sascha cries louder, sensing trouble.

I feel someone's hand on my shoulder. I look up. Miss Shelley is standing behind me in the doorway, watching.

"I think," she says, "it might be a good day for a trip. Don't you?"

———•———

I never knew there were schools as small as this. This one is way more random than my old school. We do a lot more art and a lot less maths. Plus, trips.

Today, we go to the church.

In the doorway, Miss Shelley hands everyone a clipboard and tells us to draw something.

"Find something that speaks to you and see what you can make of it." The boys all open their mouths to argue and she waves them away. "If you can't find anything exciting, you can do brass rubbings. Everyone needs more purple tombstones. Go on! Shoo! The crayons are in the box."

Miss Shelley is proper young. She's got yellow hair and long black skirts that make swishy sounds when she walks. She looks like a witch. A friendly witch who makes helpful potions from flowers and trees. She's beautiful.

She likes things that *speak to you*. I don't care. I like this church. It's dark and close and smells of crushed dust and old stone. I wonder if my dad and Auntie Meg ever came here with their school and drew something that spoke to them.

The boys have set off down the aisle.

"Look! Dead man!"

"It's a statue!"

That's Josh and Matthew. Hannah shoots them a look over her shoulder.

"Morons," she says. They ignore her. She doesn't start looking for something to draw, though. She hangs around by another statue, watching the boys.

I trail down the aisle after them, running my fingers along the top of the pews. They have little doors with ivy leaves carved in the dark wood.

Halfway down the church are two stone pillars. At the top of both is a face made of stone. A man. He's got big eyes and a long, thick nose. There are leaves sticking out of his face and his hair. He looks bright and wild, like an old god or a goblin in a fairy tale. He doesn't look like he ought to be allowed in a church.

It's the hunted man.

I stop and stare. The man last night didn't have leaves, but he had the same eyes, the same nose, the same round curve to his cheeks. It's definitely him.

"That's him!"

I'm so surprised, I say it out loud. The boys stop sliding on the stonework and stare at me.

I look for Miss Shelley.

"That man! I saw him last night, being chased."

"Was he halfway up a pillar?" says Josh.

"Did he have leaves sticking out of his nose?"

"Of course not!"

Emily has come over now, and is watching me with her quiet eyes.

"He was running away, last night!"

"You can't have seen him last night," says Josh. "That guy's been up there for years. He'd be, like, a thousand years old. He'd be a ghost."

I want to punch him. "What would you know about it anyway, Josh Haltwhistle? Were you there? How would you know who he is?"

"He's the Green Man," Miss Shelley says.

She's standing in the aisle, her dark skirt flowing and merging with her shadow, so you can't see where one begins and the other ends. The boys are silent. Even Hannah is watching.

"Is he from the Bible?" says Alexander, uncertainly.

Miss Shelley laughs. The spell is broken.

"Not exactly," she says. "'Green Man' is the name for a face like that — made of leaves or with leaves around it. It crops up in old churches and tombstones. Nobody knows why."

"Tombstones?" I say.

"Yes," she says. She looks at me. "The Green Man is linked to the cycle of death and rebirth. He's put on graves as a sign of hope."

"But people don't rebirth," says Alexander.

"Not often," says Miss Shelley. She looks so pretty I feel like melting. "OK, look. The Green Man is an old god — from before most people could read or write — so we don't really know anything about him. But people think he might have been the god of summer — or of spring. Right?"

"Right," I say. "So he's a real person, then?"

Hannah says, "It's a story, Molly." Behind her, Josh sputters into his hand. Miss Shelley shakes her head.

"It's never wise to laugh at things you don't understand," she says. "If you're not careful, they might start laughing back at you."

When the others have wandered off, I lock myself in a pew with my feet on the bench and my clipboard on my knees. I draw the man from the pillar. He's got a body of branches and hands of leaves. He has big eyes but no mouth.

I draw men on horses, with dogs and horns. The biggest is Josh and the second biggest is Matthew. They have red smiles and swords that drip red blood. They're chasing the man made of leaves. A girl with fair hair and sparkly shoes watches. She might be Emily or she might be someone else. She doesn't cheer and she doesn't cry.

"Lovely, Molly!" says Mrs. Angus, passing my pew.

6

Emily

If I could be anyone in the world, including pop stars or the queen, I would be Emily*. Emily has pink hairslides with stars on them and a set of erasers shaped like unicorns and a mum and a dad and a little brother who all live together on a farm. All the bits of her match, which they never do if you live with your grandpa and half your things are in Newcastle.

"Emily," says Hannah, "is the most boring person I have ever met. The most boring person in Britain. In the whole world!"

But Hannah is wrong. It's true that Emily doesn't say

*If I could be absolutely anyone including made-up people, I would be Pippi Longstocking, because she lives on her own with a horse and a pot of gold and a monkey called Mr. Nilsson, and if anyone tries to make her do something she doesn't want to do, like go and live with someone else, she just picks them up and carries them down the garden path and dumps them there.

And usually then they go away.

much. She hardly ever speaks in class and at break she just sits on the bench and watches, or lets Josh boss her about.

But that doesn't mean she isn't thinking things. Sometimes in class she'll say something or look at Miss Shelley in a way that shows she's listening and thinking and wondering. I try and show I'm thinking and wondering too, but I don't know if she gets it. I don't know if I'm the sort of person someone like Emily would be friends with. I'm not little and blonde — I've got short black curls that tangle, and eyes so dark they're almost black.

"You're my raggle-taggle gypsy love," says Grandpa, which is nice, but it's not much use outside of Grandpa-land.

7

Up the Lane

After school, I go up the lane on my bike. Playing outside.

Playing outside here isn't like it is at home. At home, I go and call for my best friend, Katy, or my second-best friend, Chloe, and we play badminton in the street, or build dens in Chloe's garden, or muck about on Katy's computer, or anything.

At Grandpa's, there's nobody but Hannah, and we never played much even at home. Here all we've done is fight and nearly run away. So today I'm on my own.

I take my bike out and go down the hill first, three times, for luck. Then I ride up the lane the other way, away from the village, the way I went last night.

When I get to the place with the hawthorn trees, I stop. There are dark stains on the grass that the rain hasn't washed away. They give me a shivery feeling, but I'm relieved as well.

"See!" I say, to an imaginary Josh. "He *was* real."

The imaginary Josh looks impressed.

that he's bare from the waist upward. I can see his chest muscles bulging under his brown skin.

My dad's muscles aren't anything like as good as his.

"Do you need anything?" I say. "Food? Help?"

He leans his head against the wall and smiles. It's a nice smile. Sort of tired but pleased.

"No," he says.

It reminds me of the way my mum used to look at me, half asleep as I climbed up into her bed on Sunday mornings when I was small. I come closer. I'm not sure I believe him. Coming down the lane, I'd almost convinced myself that he was Miss Shelley's god, but now I'm here, I'm doubtful. What if he's just a man, hurt like my mum was hurt?

If no one helps him, will he die too?

"Are you real?" I say suddenly.

He stretches out his hand. "There."

I go over and take his hand. The skin is rough and warm. The nails are chipped and his fingers are crumbled with dried mud and something else.

"Real," he says.

He looks exactly like the head in the church, except he doesn't have leaves. He has brown, curly hair, with strands of red and orange that glow when the sun catches them. He's wearing thick brown trousers that fold over in sort of wrinkles, like the skin of the rhinoceros in the *Just So*

Stories. They stop halfway down his leg. They're torn and mangled by the teeth of the wolves, and messed up with mud and thick-smelling blood, but if I squint and look away, I can almost forget about them.

"Your face is in our church," I say.

He doesn't seem surprised.

"Is it?" he says. He looks at me with the same fond look. Then he closes his eyes.

He's asleep.

I stay where I am for a while, watching him, but he doesn't move. I stand up, as slowly and quietly as I can, and go back to the door.

When I turn and look back, he's gone.

Really Real

I sit on top of the gate and look at the sky. *Really* real!
The way I see it, Famous Five–style, there are two
possibilities.

1. He's a real but ordinary person, unmagical. I
should (probably) dial 999 like the St. John's
Ambulance people showed us at school and rescue
him. I will be in all the newspapers — *Girl Saves
Injured Man*. I might even get a medal.
2. He's something completely different — the
Green Man and the old god from the church. And
anything could happen next.

Grandpa's serving a whole queue of customers when I
burst through the shop door. Grandma's nowhere to be
seen. Hannah's in the kitchen, kneeling on one of the
kitchen chairs. She's drawing signatures in swirly purple
letters:

Hannah Brooke
Hannah Diana Brooke
H. D. Brooke
Hannah Diana Watson-Brooke
H. D. B.
HANNAH

"Hannah. Hann*aah*."

She turns slightly but definitely round, so her back is facing me. She's turning the full stops and the dots on her "i"s into little hearts.

"Hann*aah*." I pull on her arm. "I've found him. The man from the church — the god Miss Shelley was talking about in the church. I've found where he is. We can go and rescue him!"

Hannah jerks her arm away.

"Leave me *alone*," she says. "I'm busy. I don't have time to play games."

"Hannah — I'm not messing — seriously, seriously, I've found a man, in a field. He's hurt. We can help him!"

Hannah looks ever so slightly interested.

"I honestly, honestly promise. Honestly. Swear on . . . swear on Dad's life."

"You're not supposed to swear," says Hannah, but she puts her pen down. "Show me first. Then if he's real, we'll tell Grandpa."

I lead and Hannah follows. I know I should be worried about the man, but actually I'm mostly excited to be leading a rescue mission. I wonder if we ought to have brought bandages, or at least aspirin.

"You have to climb the gate," I tell Hannah. "He's in the barn. There!"

"You didn't say there'd be *mud*!" says Hannah. She won't go straight through like I do (my school shoes couldn't get any muddier). She goes round the edge, balancing on rocks. "Ow!"

I get to the barn first. He's there, sleeping in his corner. The sun has moved, so there's a ray of light from the hole in the roof shining on his face. He looks like a curly-haired Jesus.

"Hello," I whisper. He blinks at me.

"Ough!" says Hannah. The floor inside the barn is lower than the lip of the door, and she's stepped right off it and landed on a plank of wood. She slides off and grabs my arm. "What *is* this place?"

"It's where he is." I point. "Look."

"Where?" says Hannah. "What're you pointing at?"

I look.

But he's gone.

Mum

I want Mum tonight. I want to tell her about the man in the barn. I want to take her there and say, "A man was here and then he wasn't. Is he real?"

"The world is a strange and wonderful place, Molly-love."

That's what she'd say.

"The world is a strange and wonderful place," I whisper, but it just makes me feel more alone than ever.

From my bed, I can see the light on the landing. I can hear people laughing on the television. I could go and talk to Grandma and Grandpa. I could tell them a hunt rode through our village last night. A huntsman rode through our village and was gone. I could say there's a man in a barn and he's hurt. But I'm going to save him.

I don't move.

My mum's name was Diana Eleanor Brooke. She died on the eighth of August. She was thirty-nine, which sounds very old, but isn't really. Not when you think that Grandma is sixty-nine and Grandpa is seventy-four.

My mum was the most beautiful person in the whole world, probably. Beautifuller than Miss Shelley, even. She had long, fair hair and green witch-eyes and a turned-up nose with freckles, which is a most un-adult thing to have. Neither Hannah nor I look much like her. When I was little, I used to hope that my black curls would turn blond and straight and so one day I might grow up to look like her, but it never happened. The only thing we have in common is freckles. She was the only grown-up I ever saw with freckles. She wasn't ever very like a grown-up, though. She was grown-up about things like bedtimes and cleaning your teeth, but she was like a little kid about other things, like Christmas trees and fireworks and fairies. She believed in fairies. She thought she'd seen one once, when she was smaller than me. Only it was just for a moment, out of a car window, so she was never sure. I almost believe in fairies too. And I like Christmas trees, and banana ice cream, and jumping waves at the seaside, like she did.

Mum is the person I want now. She's the person I want to tell about my man. She wouldn't think I was playing games or making things up, like Grandma and Hannah do. She'd know what to do. She'd —

I don't know what she'd do, but she'd believe me.

11

Flower and Tree

So I'm on my own. That's OK. When I come home from school, I go straight through to the kitchen. The shop would be a better place to go, but Grandma's in there and, anyway, she'd notice if things went missing. The kitchen is Grandpa's place and he's much less observant. I get a carrier bag from the drawer and I fill it with things. Apples. Bread. Orange juice. A packet of ham. A tin of beans, a tin of peaches, a tin of thick rice and tomato soup. A fork. Matches.

If nobody else is going to help him, that doesn't mean I can't.

There are blackberries growing in the hedgerows in the lane. More of the trees are turning autumn colored — soft yellows and oranges. It looks as if somebody's smudged over the world with a paintbrush, dulling and mixing the colors. The banks are covered in the hard stalks of dead cow parsley. The air is fresher, and colder. It smells of leaves and grass and wet earth.

When I go through into the barn, he's there. He's awake. He's moved. Last time he was leaning against the wall; now he's huddled up in the corner, out of the wind.

"Hello," I say.

He looks up when I come in. "Molly, isn't it?" he says. "I wondered if you were coming back." He holds out his hand and I come and sit beside him.

In the evening light, I can see his legs clearly. They look awful. I can see the stains and tears, all the way down. There's a strong smell, like something's rotting, and flies are crawling about on his strange trousers. I look away.

"Do they hurt?" I say.

He yawns and shakes his head again.

"Should I get an ambulance? Someone to help?"

"An ambulance wouldn't find me," he says.

We sit there quiet together, watching the dust dancing in the sunlight from the door.

"I've brought you some stuff," I say. "I thought you might — I mean, if you want — you don't have to have them if you don't want them."

I pass the carrier bag over to him. He looks at it, puzzled, and pulls out a tin of peaches. He turns the tin around, sniffs at it. His mouth gives a funny twitch at the picture, then he lays it on the ground.

"It's pretty," he says. "Thank you."

"It's a tin of peaches!" I say. "Don't you know what a tin is?"

He looks at me, expectant. I tug at the ring-pull and open the tin for him.

"Look. Peaches."

He dips a grimy finger into the peach juice and touches his tongue to it, cautious. I watch him. A look of surprise crosses his face and he laughs out loud.

"It's sweet!"

"You can eat it. I brought you a fork — look."

But he doesn't want the fork. He digs his fingers into the syrup and eats the peach slices whole, juice running down his chin. I know exactly what Grandma would say about eating with hands as dirty as his, but he seems happy.

He shakes his head when I show him the rest of the food in the bag.

"Enough. It's enough. Thank you."

"Aren't you hungry?" I say, and he shakes his head.

I'm puzzling over this when I notice something else. Something is growing out of the soil beside him. A tree. A baby tree. A sapling.

It's almost as tall as him. And I'm almost certain it wasn't there last time.

"Where did that come from?"

He looks up, lifts his hand, and touches the branch above his head. It *grows* — I swear it — stretching out like it wants to wrap itself around his fingers. He draws his hand down and the new branch follows.

And I notice other things. There's grass growing around his feet that wasn't there before. And the ivy crawling up the wall — there's more of it behind him. Was it always like that? Or —

He sees me staring and laughs. He holds out his hands. They're empty. He blows on them and something begins to grow, out of nothing. A seed. A little green sprout. Leaves. A flower.

A bluebell.

"For you," he says and gives the flower to me.

I hold the bluebell very carefully in the palm of my hand. I'm afraid it'll vanish if I move.

He's watching my face. He seems pleased. He sits back. "No," he says. "I don't need your food."

12

Jack

When I come back, Jack's raking our garden. I stand on the gate and watch.

Jack lives next door to the shop, with Ivy. Ivy's a bit batty. She shuffles around all day in slippers and a pink hat with flowers on it. She's not supposed to go beyond the garden, but sometimes she escapes and wanders down the lane and Jack has to go and bring her home. Once, I saw her escaping and ran after her and brought her back. Jack was in the kitchen and he said, "Eh, lass, where were you off to this time?" She looked up and beamed this great big beam, with no teeth in it, and said, "I was going to the circus!"

I like Ivy.

I like Jack better, though. Jack's a man, but he does all their cooking and cleaning. He even washes Ivy in the bath. He told me so. Jack and Grandma and Grandpa have a big garden between them, and Jack looks after it.

He rests his chin on his rake when he sees me, and raises his hand.

"What's up, woodchuck?"

"Nothing," I say. I climb over the gate and sit on top of it. Jack carries on raking.

"I've got a flower," I tell him.

"Have you?"

"A bluebell."

I've got it in my pocket if he wants to see, but he doesn't ask. He carries on raking.

"That's a brave bluebell," he says. "Out in October."

"It's magic," I say. "A man made it grow out of nothing."

Jack doesn't answer. He rakes his leaves into a pile.

"You believe me, don't you?" I say. "You do believe in magic?"

Jack stops.

"Do you see those trees?" He points. I nod. "I made them grow out of nothing." He laughs. "There's more magic in trees than in conjuring tricks," he says.

13

Wish Upon an Oak God

I go back into the house. I'm thinking a thought. Not a big one. It's right at the back of my head, so small that I don't dare bring it into the light or even think it in anything but a sidelong sort of way. If I do, it might crumble away to nothing, the way things do sometimes when you show them to someone else.

The thought is this: If the man in the barn *is* a god, and if he brings the summer, and plucks growing things out of the air, and does whatever else a summer god does, *what else can he do?*

Not superpowers or jewels or fairy palaces. I don't want these things. My wishes are simple and plain.

Could he make my dad take us back?

Could he bring my mum home safe?

14

Un-Quality Time

He does something to my head, this man. When I go and see him, I forget all the things I ought to ask — like *Who are you?* — and get distracted by bare feet and ivy leaves.

I don't even know his name. If I was one of the Famous Five, I'd have solved this mystery by now.

Of course, if I was one of the Famous Five, he'd be either a smuggler or a gypsy or a detective in disguise.

But still.

On Saturday, at breakfast, I make a list of all the questions I want answered, starting with *What is your name?* and working my way through *Are you really a pagan god?* right up to *What else can you do besides make trees? And could you teach me how, so I can do it too?*

"Can I go out?" I ask Grandpa, but he shakes his head.

"Not today, lovey."

What's today? Another day out with Auntie Meg or one of Mum's friends? Going to "play" with my cousins, who are boys and at secondary school and like computers and football and stare at us like they've forgotten how to talk?

"Your dad's taking you out, love. Remember?"

Oh. Dad.

"Molly Alice," says Grandma, putting down the butter knife. "Don't look like that. You want to see your dad, don't you?"

"Yes," I say. I scratch the plastic tabletop with my fingernail. "Of course I do."

"I don't," says Hannah. She spears her fork into her egg and glares at Grandpa.

He looks away.

Every time Dad comes, I look forward and look forward to it, and every time it's horrible.

We're in a car park. Hannah is scrunched as far toward the other side of the car as she can get. She's got her earphones plugged in and her music turned up as far as it will go.

"Come on, love," says Dad. "Come and have something to eat."

"Leave me alone!"

Dad is crouched by the door. You can tell he doesn't know what to do. Mum usually does all the talking and fighting in our family.

I'm standing next to him looking out over the car park.

I feel like we've been here for *hours*. I wish he would just tell her what a brat she's being. Someone (not me) ought to.

"Can't we just leave her here, Dad? I'm hungry."

"Oh, grow up," Hannah snarls, sudden as I imagine tigers might be. "And keep your nose out of other people's business."

Dad rocks back. He opens his mouth, then, all of a sudden, he shuts it again. He stands up and strides out across the car park, without looking back at either of us.

I run after him. Hannah's *always* horrible on days Dad takes us out. Last time he took us to the Harry Potter castle in Alnwick and she sang "I know a song that'll get on your nerves" all round the tour. The time before that we went to the beach and she tipped sand over his seat and all the sandwiches because he said we couldn't have fish and chips.

Today, she won't even get out of the car.

I catch up with Dad at the café queue. We're supposed to be looking round some old house with gardens. I don't know why. Dad hates gardens. And the only old house I like is Newby Hall, because of the paddleboats and the zip line.

I rub Dad's elbow to show him I'm there. He gives me a quick smile, but it vanishes immediately.

"What do you want to eat?" he says. "There're sandwiches over there — look. Go and choose something."

It's no wonder he doesn't want to have us, if all that happens when he comes is that we fight. I go and pick out a plasticky cheese sandwich from the fridge, with horrible slimy-looking pickle in it.

It's cold.

Dad takes a seat right over from the window, like he doesn't care about Hannah. But he keeps looking over his shoulder at the car. It's not fair. This is my day with Dad just as much as hers.

I take a sugar lump from the bowl and bite on it. I expect him to tell me off, but he doesn't even notice.

"Can't we leave Hannah behind next time?" I say, to make him look at me. "She's *always* horrible."

Dad rubs his face with his hands.

"Hannah's not horrible," he says. "Any more than you are, or me. She's . . ." He hesitates, like he's trying to think of a nice way to say "horrible." "Well," he says. "This isn't easy for anyone."

Rubbing your face means you're tired. Is Dad tired? I don't know. He's older than other people's dads. And uglier. His hair is thin and turning gray at the edges, and his face is all squashed up and lopsided, like a pug dog's.

"I don't know why you ever took up with him,"

Grandma used to grumble to Mum when she was ticked off with him. And Mum would lean across the table, her face teasing, and say, "He made me laugh, of course."

Suddenly, I want him back very much.

"Maybe we should come and live with you," I say. "Then Hannah wouldn't be so huffy all the time."

"I wish you could, sweetheart," says Dad. But his eyes don't come alive when he says it.

"We could!" I say. I lean forward. "I don't care how much you work. Me and Hannah can look after ourselves. We could cook you meals and everything."

I can cook. I can make tea and coffee and peppermint creams and chocolate crispy cakes and soup and beans on toast and sandwiches. That's enough to live on.

But Dad is shaking his head.

"No, sweetheart," he says. "Don't let's start this again. You can't stay in the house on your own and neither can Hannah. Not at night. And with this job, I can't guarantee I'll be around."

This is unbelievably unfair. Loads of kids Hannah's age stay at home on their own. And kids look after their parents, if they're in a wheelchair or something. I saw a *Blue Peter* about it.

"You could get a babysitter," I say. "I wouldn't care. Or a childminder, or an after-school club — lots of people do."

"Moll," says Dad wearily. "Don't let's fight about this now. You can't ask babysitters to come at the sort of notice I can give. And you can't stay overnight at a childminder's."

Cold shivers down my spine.

"But we're going to come back with you," I say. "You said! You *promised*! We can't live with Grandpa *forever*!"

Dad closes his eyes and I stop, frightened. He's leaving again. Would he just walk away from me, the way he did from Hannah? I catch my breath, but then his eyes open again.

"Not forever, sweetheart," he says. "I can't have you right now, Moll. I can barely look after myself. Once I've found another job, we'll look at it then."

I'm angry at him for making me so frightened, and for spoiling my happy day. It's not fair. Dads are supposed to want their kids to have a good time.

"So find a job!" I say. "You just have to fill in a form or go to an interview or something. It takes about five minutes! It doesn't take weeks and weeks and weeks like this!"

"I'm trying," says Dad. "I really am, sweetheart."

"Try harder. Everyone else has jobs. It's not hard!"

Dad used to wind Mum up something rotten by not fighting with her, and he's doing it to me now. It's as if there's a wall around him, and he won't let any of my words get through.

"Come on," he says. "Let's go back to Hannah. Let's see if she'll let us into the car."

In the car, Hannah's face is screwed up like she's trying not to cry. Dad passes her a packet of slimy cheese sandwiches and she opens them without saying anything. He turns the car round and we head back to the village.

When we get to Grandpa's house, Hannah bolts out of the door and runs inside. Dad gives this sort of sad shrug, like he doesn't know what to do. Dads are *supposed* to know what to do! That's their job!

"Come on, love," he says wearily, putting his hand on my shoulder. I pull away and run through the shop door, past Grandpa and up the stairs.

Sometimes I know just what it feels like to be Hannah.

Sometimes I hate Dad too.

15

Dad

There are two reasons why we don't live with Dad.

The first is his job. Dad's a journalist, which means that people, i.e., his boss, keep ringing him up and saying, "We need you to cover a story in Shepley, sharpish." And then he has to drive all the way to Shepley and find out about whatever the story is* and then he doesn't get home till late, sometimes not till after we're in bed.

The second reason is that after Mum died, Dad got sort of ill too. He went and worked twice as late, every night (Auntie Rose was staying, so he could leave us). And sometimes he would come home and stare at nothing and not answer when you tried to talk to him, which is scary when homeless people do it, but doubly, triply, quadruply scary when the person doing it is your own dad. And Auntie Rose did all the important things, like

*Not exciting stories. More things like people winning cleanest toilet competitions, or hospitals not spending money on what they're supposed to.

buy food, but all the extra things like piano lessons and school shoes got forgotten about. Then one day Grandma came, because Auntie Rose had to go and see her own kids, and he started crying, right there in the kitchen, and Grandma told me to go outside, but I listened anyway, and I heard her say, "You know we're always happy to have the children, Toby."

And when Grandma said that, it was as if there were two bits of me. One bit was excited — because I like Grandma, and I particularly like Grandpa, and there's something grand and adventurous about living in the country with your grandparents, like being evacuated with a label round your neck. But the other bit of me knew that the only reason it was exciting was because it would never happen. Because I couldn't ever believe, really, that a dad like ours, a good dad, who loves us and doesn't lock us in cupboards or forget to feed us, would ever really abandon us.

But he did.

16

A Mizzle Full of Questions

After Dad's gone, I come and stand in the shop door. It's raining again. Not bucketing, cats-and-dogsy rain, but a shivery, drizzly rain with flecks of silver in it, so thin you can hardly be sure it's there. It hangs in tiny droplets on the edge of the roof, and on my sleeve when I hold it out.

"A drizzle," I say out loud.

"A mizzle," says Grandpa. "A mizzle's finer."

Mizzling. We're in the mizzle of a mizzle.

"Can I go out?" I say. "I found where the man is — the one who vanished into nothing. He's hiding in a little house. He's growing flowers."

"All right," says Grandpa. I'm still not sure he believes me. "But try and stay dry."

"I like being wet," I say.

"All right for you, curly-mop," says Grandpa. He comes and stands behind me in the door. We watch the rain.

"Don't be too angry with your dad," he says suddenly. "He's doing his best."

I tip my head back and look up at him, surprised. He kisses my forehead.

"Go on," he says. "Go and find your fella. Before I change my mind."

Everything looks different in a mizzle. Like in a mist. The trees the farthest away I can see are almost invisible. Inmizzible.

I push open the barn door very, very slowly.

"Hello?"

He's there.

He's moved again. He's had to. His tree's grown. It's not a sapling anymore: It's a proper little tree. The top branches hang above the tumbledown top of the wall. There are little leaves, all covered in mizzle-beads. Oak leaves, like picture-book clouds.

The ivy's grown too. It stretches across half the back wall. Little yellow flowers are pushing their way through the floor. He's sitting with his back against the trunk of the tree. He looks bright and strange and wild-looking — and somehow older than he did before. I can't work him out at all. At home, I think maybe he's a tramp or an escaped prisoner or something, but here I really believe he's a god, like Miss Shelley says.

I take out my notebook and start right at the beginning.

"What's your name?"

He frowns.

"Like, I'm Molly. Who are you?"

"I don't have a name like Molly," he says. "Why should I?"

He doesn't say it angry, like Hannah would, but curious. Like he really doesn't know what I mean.

The next question on my list is *Are you the god of summer?* but somehow now I'm here I don't dare ask it. I try something else.

"How old are you?"

If he *is* Miss Shelley's god, he was only born in the spring.

"Older than an acorn."

"Have you ever seen a winter?"

"A winter? Why? Have you lost one?"

"One's coming soon. Then you'll be cold."

He gives me his most loving look.

"I don't get cold."

I rest my chin on the top of my knees and wrap my arms around them. *I'm* cold. Even here under the roof, the rain still catches me when the wind blows in.

"Why can't anyone else see you? Why do you keep disappearing?"

"Do you mind?" he says. "I don't want to worry you."

"I . . ." I don't know what to say. He reaches out his hand and touches mine. I shiver.

"I don't want them to find me," he says.

"The hunt people?"

He doesn't answer. "You are being careful," he says instead. "Aren't you? Nights are getting longer. The Holly King's getting stronger. . . ."

"The Holly King," I say. "Who's he?" But I already know the answer. "He's the man on the horse, isn't he? The one who was leading the hunt? The one who's after you?"

He closes his eyes again.

"Don't be frightened," he says. "I don't want to frighten you."

"He couldn't hurt me," I say. "Could he?"

"Of course he could." He looks surprised that I could even ask such a question. "Perhaps you shouldn't come anymore," he says. "I don't want him to hurt you. . . ."

"Would he?" I say. He doesn't answer. "He wants to hurt you," I say. "Doesn't he?"

My man watches me without moving, leaning back against the tree.

"Yes," he says. "He wants to hurt me."

We're quiet. I'm filled with uncertainty, mingled with fear. Surely he can't just mean to sit here, waiting for the Holly King to come? Surely he's going to do something?

"Can't you use magic on him?"

"Magic?"

"Like you used to make my flower."

"Your flower made itself," he says.

"Can you make other things make themselves?" I say hopefully.

He starts to laugh and then it turns into coughing, horrible, wet coughing, and I'm frightened. I don't think he can stop, but he does, eventually.

"Are you all right?" I say.

He shakes his head. I wonder if I ought to go. But he holds out his hand like he wants me to stay.

"You can do so much stuff," I say. I'm thinking of all the things that go with spring: celandines in the field behind Grandpa's house, baby blackbird beaks opening and closing in their nest in our plum tree, spider silk shining on the grass in the mornings. "Can —" I stop. "Do you make baby animals get born?"

He holds out his hand again, thoughtfully, turning it so that the palm is upward. I wonder if he's going to make something for me — a baby mouse, maybe, or a squirrel, perhaps. I'd like a squirrel. He must have guessed what I'm thinking because he looks up, and his eyes are laughing. "You can't make a baby without a mother, can you?" he says, teasing. Ivy curls out of the palm of his hand and up his arm. He holds up his hand, watching it.

The muscles in my chest tighten. I look down at the earth. "Could you make the mother too?" I say quietly. "Could you make someone come alive for me, if I asked you? Only, your face is on tombstones, my teacher said. You're the god of rebirth, she said. Someone dead — could you make them come alive? Could you?"

He doesn't answer. I look up. But he's gone again.

17

Long Distance

Dad rings this evening.

"Are you all right, love?" he says.

I nod, then remember that he can't see me. "Yes," I say.

"Sorry I was so rotten, love," he says. He sounds tired, like most of him is somewhere else. "I'm doing my best."

"I know," I say. I lean my head against the wall. "I'm sorry too."

"Peace?"

"Peace."

We're quiet. I tap my heels against the stair, waiting for him to say something.

"Did you have a good afternoon?" he says eventually.

"I went to see my man," I tell him. "This man I've met. He lives in a little house, like in a book, because he's hiding from this hunt who are trying to kill him. He can make things out of nothing, like trees and flowers and magic potions."

"Sounds useful," says Dad. "Maybe you can introduce me next time I come and see you."

"Maybe," I say doubtfully. "Only he won't let anyone but me see him. He makes himself invisible."

"Oh well," says Dad. He gives a little half-laugh, although I can't see what's so funny.

Hannah puts her head round the kitchen door.

"Dinner!" she says.

I cover the phone with my hand.

"D'you want to talk to Dad?"

Hannah shakes her head and vanishes.

"I've got to go," I say.

"All right," Dad says. He draws in his breath. "Don't I get a kiss?"

I kiss my fingers and press them against the phone.

"There. Did you get it?"

"Wait —" says Dad. "Yes — no — no — oh, yes! There! Got it!"

"Your turn."

"OK," says Dad. I can hear him smiling. "Sending now. Ready?"

I squeeze my eyes shut and wait for the time it takes a kiss to travel all the way from Newcastle down a phone line. The kiss zips down wires and across space.

It shoots through the receiver and lands on my cheek with a splat.

"Got it?" says Dad.

"Yes," I say. "Got it."

"Off you go, then," says Dad. He sounds suddenly sad. I put the phone down, so I don't have to hear.

18

Golden Leaves and Kings

The leaves on the trees are changing color, turning from green to yellow and falling from the sky. They do it at home too, only you don't notice because there aren't so many of them. There are rosehips in the hedges and red berries on the hawthorn bushes, a cold tang in the air and fallen leaves to crunch through in the grass.

In school one morning, a great wind blows up. We all go out and try and catch the leaves as they swirl down from the trees in the road. We gather them up and take them back to press in dictionaries and atlases. On Wednesday, we take them out and laminate them and turn them into mobiles to hang from the ceiling. Mrs. Angus — who turns out to know a lot about trees — teaches us the Latin names, which we'd never have learned in my old school. Oak — *Quercus robur*. Ash — *Fraxinus excelsior*. Hawthorn — *Crataegus monogyna*.

I like to think that they're the real name of the tree, the friendly name you'd use if it ever happened to speak to you. Quercus Robur sounds funny and friendly. Fraxinus Excelsior is brave, like a knight. Crataegus Monogyna is a little frightening, a shriveled-up old witch-tree with long red fingers.

We don't do holly, which is good, because I don't want anything from the Holly King in my book. I ask Miss Shelley about him, though.

"The Holly King?" she says. "Where did you hear about him?"

"The man was talking about him. You remember — I told you. The statue from the church, that I met."

Across the table, Josh whispers something to Matthew and Matthew sputters. Miss Shelley ignores them.

"I see," she says. "Well, the Holly King is another pagan archetype. He's a counterbalance to the Oak King — which is another name for your Green Man. The Oak King rules in spring and summer and the Holly King in autumn and winter."

So my man's the good one and the Holly King's the evil one.

"Do they fight?" I say. "Is that what counterbalance means — that they're enemies?"

"Sort of," says Miss Shelley. "Look, Molly, it's all rather complicated. There are so many stories —"

But the Holly King's not a story! Why can't anyone understand this? He's a real person, and he's after my man. The Green Man or the Oak King or whatever his name is.

Miss Shelley's watching me. So's Emily, across the table.

"The Holly King kills him," I say. "He does, doesn't he?"

"In some versions of the story," Miss Shelley says. "Yes. The Holly King and the Oak King fight at midwinter and the Holly King defeats the Oak King."

I clench my lips, tight as oak roots.

"Molly?" says Miss Shelley.

I look up.

"Does he have a hunt?" I say.

"A hunt?"

"A wild hunt? Does the Holly King have one?"

"Oh, the wild hunt," says Miss Shelley. "All sorts of people had a wild hunt, Molly. Woden and Odin, Herne, of course — the Devil in some versions — King Arthur in others. Even your Green Man is supposed to lead it, in some stories."

"He doesn't!" I say. "He wouldn't!"

Matthew snorts. Behind Miss Shelley's head, Josh makes circling motions around his ear. *Crazy.*

"You stop that!" I say. Miss Shelley jumps.

"Molly!"

"It was Josh!" I say.

At break, Hannah corners me.

"Why do you have to do that?" she says, pushing me back against the playground wall. "Why do you have to go on about hunts and stupid gods? Everyone thinks you're mad. You do know that, don't you? If you have to make up stories, at least pick ones that make sense."

"It's *not* a story," I say, furious. Hannah glares.

"Grow up," she says. She drops her hands and walks away.

I feel tears starting in the back of my eyes. Hannah's supposed to be my sister. Sisters are supposed to stick up for each other.

"Mum would have believed me," I call after her.

She doesn't look back.

19

An Aneurysm in the Family

An aneurysm is this disease that people get sometimes. It's where the wall of one of your blood
vessels gets damaged, so blood flows into the wall and
makes a balloon, which gets bigger and bigger until it
explodes inside you and you die.

Aneurysms can happen to anyone at any time — even
kids can get them, though Auntie Rose says it's not very
likely me or Hannah will. She says they only happen
really, really rarely. Also, mostly people who get them are
old. So out of the people I know, Grandpa is most likely
to get one, because he's the oldest.

Which means he's probably going to be the next person I love to die.

An aneurysm is what happened to Mum. It's why she
died. She waved us off at the school gate and then got
into her car and drove off, and half an hour later she was
dead. So we were the last people to see her alive.

Probably, if we'd been doctors, or the Famous Five, or
if we'd known about aneurysms, we would have noticed

something was wrong and saved her. You would think that if someone is about to die in half an hour, her children would notice. But we didn't.

When it happened they rang Dad at work, but they didn't ring us. We only found out when we came out of school and Grandma was standing there waiting for us. But by then she was already dead.

So we never even got to say good-bye.

20

A Man in the Lane

Kick. Kick. Kick. I stump down the lane, kicking up leaves. You don't know what you're talking about, Hannah. Neither do you, smelly Josh Haltwhistle. Kick. Neither do you, Dad. You could have us back if you wanted. You could.

I stamp around the corner . . .

. . . and stop.

He's there. A tall figure, snuffling around the lane.

I shrink back in the hedge. He's got his back to me, looking down at the track to my man's house. He's so close that I could throw a stone and hit him.

It's the huntsman. The Holly King.

From behind the hedge, I stare. In the daylight, he looks half-human, thick and stooped and low, with strange, high shoulders and legs that look more like a bull's than a man's. He's wearing some sort of cloak, but his legs are covered in thick black hair, like a faun's. His face, when he turns it to look down the lane, is human enough, though it's flatter and wider than a normal face, and his horns are gone. He's got that same . . . wildness about him that my man has. He looks like someone who's stepped out of a story, not the sort of somebody you'd meet just walking into Grandpa's shop to buy stamps.

I creep slowly backward. He's staring down the track toward the field where my man is. Does he know he's there? Why doesn't he go in after him?

What's he waiting for?

I edge down the lane, secret-agent-style, and round the corner. There's another field here. I climb over the gate and now I start to run.

His field should be behind this one. Behind or along. I duck under the electric shock wire and look round. Here is a bigger field, longer, bumpier, with marshy clumps of yellow grass and spindly trees. I'm not sure how it joins on to the field where my man is. I think his field is . . . over there.

I run across, wellies squashing into the marshiness. When I get to the wall, I stop.

This is his field all right. The trees are moving. Back and forth, back and forth, like there's a hurricane blowing.

I stumble-run across to his barn.

"Man! Man!"

He's not there.

"Man!"

I run out of the barn and all the way around the back of it, in case he's hiding.

He's not.

"Man!" I run back inside. He's gone. He's not in any of the corners, or hiding behind the sacks or the rubbish in the corner. His oak tree is rustling and shaking, orangey leaves falling like water from a dog. I'm ankle deep in dead leaves.

"Man!"

I run back out.

"Molly —"

He's standing up against the wall, holding on to the door frame. He's shaking like the tree inside, shaking so much that I'm sure he's going to fall.

"He's here! In the lane! The Holly —"

I reach for his hand, and he grabs it and squeezes my fingers so tight that I think my bones are going to snap.

"Don't," he says. "Shh."

I can feel how tense he is. I can feel the tenseness in his hand and it frightens me. This isn't my strong wood god.

"Is he coming to get you?" I whisper. He looks down at me and rubs my arm.

"No," he says. "Not yet."

Not yet.

"Help me," he says, and at first I don't understand

what he means. But then he puts his arm across my shoulders and I realize.

He leans on me and I hold him up. He's heavier than I expected; a warm, shaking weight against my arm. The scent of him is stronger again and I clench my nose shut. Together — step by step — we make our way back in the barn.

Inside, he collapses into the leaves around the oak tree, which gives this little shiver and stops shaking. It's a proper tree now, with branches reaching up through the hole in the roof. He leans his head back against it and closes his eyes. He's pale, under his tan. The gashes on his legs have opened again. I can see purple and black bruises on his skin and a mess of dried blood and pus around the wounds and on his ragged trousers.

I realize I'm shaking too.

"Why isn't he coming now?" I say. "Why's he after you? What did you do to him?"

He doesn't open his eyes.

"Tell me!" I say. "Tell me now! Don't leave again!"

He shakes his head against the tree trunk.

"Stay here! Don't go! Why isn't he coming?"

"The sun . . ."

"What's the sun got to do with anything?"

I want to shake him. His skin is a grayish color, bluish-white around his lips.

"No," he says.

"No what?"

"I can't stay here anymore," he says, and he's fading. He's fading. I clutch at him, but he's gone, leaving me with nothing but the oak tree and the fallen leaves.

The tree shudders, and is still.

In the lane, the man-thing — the Holly King — is standing upright at the edge of the track, like he's stepped down from a real magical kingdom somewhere. I can see leaves fluttering down from the tree above his head. It's barer now than the others in the lane. The grass around his clawed feet is white with frost, thick where he stands, fading as it spreads away and out. As I watch, beads of frost creep up the branch of the tree, pale and icy. I shiver.

Around me, it's growing dark.

21

Demeter

How does a god change the weather?

I know another story about winter.

It's about a Greek goddess whose little girl vanishes. One minute she's playing in the forest, the next she's gone.

The goddess wanders the whole world over, searching for her daughter, whose name is Persephone. She's so sad that everything stops growing. Leaves fall out of the trees. Flowers put their heads out of the ground and shrivel back into the earth. Nothing grows, so nobody has anything to eat and everyone is hungry.

One day, when she's searching by a river, the goddess finds her daughter's belt on the ground. She picks it up and starts crying all over again.

As she's sitting there, this woman's head pokes up out of the stream. It's a water nymph.

"Woman," says the nymph. "Stop crying. Your daughter is Queen in the Underworld. Hades, Lord of the Dead, has stolen her and made her his bride."

When the goddess hears that, she leaps up and flies straight to Zeus, who's King of the Gods and Persephone's father.

"Zeus," she says, bowing low. "Please help. Please save our daughter."

But Zeus is angry. He's angry because nothing will grow, because his people are dying.

"What do you have against my brother, King of the Underworld?" he says. "Persephone is as great a queen there as my wife is here."

(So Persephone has married her uncle. But that sort of thing was quite normal for Greek gods, so no one cared.)

Persephone's mother carries on crying and pleading. And in the end, Zeus gives in.

"She may go free," he says, "so long as she has eaten none of the fruit of the Underworld."

Up jumps the goddess, laughing with joy. But Zeus gets the last laugh. Because Persephone has eaten eight pomegranate seeds in Hades' garden, so she has to stay.

Hades doesn't want his wife to be unhappy, though, so he makes a deal. Persephone gets to spend six months with her mother on Earth and six months with him in the Underworld. And that's why the Greeks thought we had summer and winter — winter because Persephone's mother is so sorry she's gone, and summer because she's so pleased to have her back.

I like that story. I think it's true, that being sad makes things darker and colder, but being happy makes them bright.

Persephone's mother is called Demeter.

She's the goddess of motherly love and things that grow.

22

King Conkers

At the end of the school road, there's a big conker tree. In school today, the boys are full of it.

"Miss, the conkers are out!"

"Miss, can we go get conkers?"

"Miss, it's educational, miss!"

At my old school, conkers weren't educational. They were Violent and Competitive and If You Can't Play Nicely, You Can't Play At All. Here, though, Miss Shelley takes us down the road at break time and we pick as many as we can. Josh and Matthew get loads, whole conker battalions full. Alexander gets three — the biggest he can find.

In class we learn about conkers. Their long name is horse chestnuts, but you don't roast them on a fire. They're seeds. There's a little spark of life inside each one, sleeping until spring. The ones that land in the right place, when spring comes, a little shoot pops out of the top of them. And then the shoot grows and grows until it's turned into a whole new conker tree.

Or that's what Miss Shelley says, at least.

None of the boys care about shoots and trees. At lunch, they all rush to the Art Table and start fighting over who gets to use the screwdrivers and drills. The poor conkers get hung on bits of art string and taken outside to get bashed.

Alexander's gets bashed by Matthew.

Matthew's gets bashed by Josh.

So does Sascha's, which is kind of unfair because Sascha's only six. But Mrs. Angus says Josh has to let her play, so really it's her fault.

Josh's conker is a *three-er*.

Josh's conker wins everything. It smashes Alexander's second conker and two more of Matthew's. Now it's a *six-er*.

Josh roams around the playground, looking for more things to bash.

"You got a conker?" he says to me. I shake my head. My conkers are undrilled, safe in my pocket.

"You got one?" he says to Hannah. Hannah's on the bench at the edge of the playground. She's listening to Dad's iPod like she doesn't care what anyone else is doing. She pulls the earplugs out of her ears and makes Josh ask over again.

"Conker," says Josh. "You got one?"

"Conkers are for kids," says Hannah. Josh goes red.

"You drilled yours," he says. "I *saw* you."

Hannah stands up. She's taller than Josh in her platform shoes.

"Go on, then," she says.

Josh had first whack on all the others, but Hannah doesn't give him a chance. She's got her conker pulled back ready to fight. Josh opens his mouth, then shuts it again.

Hannah narrows her eyes. She pulls back the conker string and lets fly. Josh's conker swings back, but it's all right.

It's Josh's go now. He screws up his face and pulls back his string. Whack! But Hannah's conker is all right too.

Hannah's getting into it now. This time, when she whacks Josh's conker, a bit flies off the edge. She gets another go. A whole chunk of Josh's conker breaks off. It falls off the thread. Hannah's won.

"There," she says.

Josh's face is bright red. He looks like Sascha did when he broke her conker, just before she started to cry.

"Cheat," he says. "You *cheated*. You must have done!"

Over by the school door, Oliver is ringing the bell. *Ding*dong, *ding*dong, *ding*dong.

"Line up, everyone!" calls Mrs. Angus.

"Cheat!" says Josh.

Hannah gives him this *look*. She doesn't bother to reply. She just picks up the iPod and marches over to the line.

Josh scowls.

"Your sister's a bloody cheat," he says. "And you're a moron."

Alexander's at the back of the line with his last conker. It's the best one, a king conker, big and shiny.

"Don't fight Hannah," I say. "She'll only win."

Alexander looks at his conker fondly.

"I'm not going to fight anyone," he says. "I'm going to plant it like Miss Shelley said. Then I'll have a conker tree of my own."

I look at Alexander's conker.

"It's got a hole drilled in it."

"So?" says Alexander. "I'll take out the string."

"Will it grow with a hole in it?"

Alexander shrugs.

"Maybe it'll grow pre-drilled conkers!"

When I get back to my room, I take out my conkers and line them up on my windowsill. There are four. Tinker, tailor, soldier, sailor. I lay my head on the sill and look at them sideways.

I could drill them up and let Hannah bash them all.

Or I could plant them and grow them into conker trees in the spring.

23

Empty

I go back to his barn this evening. I call and call, then I go out into the field and call, then I come back to the barn and I call again.

He doesn't answer.

He doesn't come.

He's gone too.

24

A State of Terror

The rain gushes down the windows and pours down the hill. My hair is plastered to my skull as I fight my way back down the lane. It's a proper stream already. A Molly Brook.

Grandma's serving Jack when I come through the shop door.

"She's a little madam," she's saying. "I don't know how much longer —"

She breaks off as she sees me. "And where have you been, miss?"

"Out. On my bike."

"All right. Go and take your wellies off, then. Don't trail mud through the house. And don't wake your grandpa up!"

She doesn't say anything about me being so wet. Or why I've been out so long that the light has almost gone and the sky is gray and heavy with night and rain.

I go and pull off my wellies in the hall. I can hear sounds from the kitchen. Crashing.

"And the other one —" Grandma's saying.

I hesitate. There's a smashing noise from the kitchen.

I open the kitchen door and stop. The floor is covered in broken glass and bits of bowls and plates. Hannah's standing on a chair with her head in the back of the top cupboard. When she hears me, she turns, hands wrapped around Grandpa's extra-large casserole dish.

"*Hannah!*"

Hannah gives me her flintiest, don't-try-and-stop-me look. She holds the casserole dish high over the side of the chair. Then she lets go.

I scream and jump back. Bits of ex-casserole dish go skidding across the floor.

"Han*naah*! Stop it! What are you *doing*?"

"I want to go home," says Hannah. She says it very calmly. She picks a mug off the mug-tree.

"*Hannah!*" Grandma's come through from the shop. She stands in the doorway beside me for a moment, staring at the mess, then she's across the room, grabbing Hannah by the wrist and wrenching the mug out of her hand. Then she slaps her across the face.

Hannah gasps. No one has ever smacked us, ever, no matter what we did. I'm not even sure it's legal. Grandma grabs her by the wrists, and Hannah struggles to free herself, the chair rocking back against the cupboard.

"Stop it!" I shriek. "Stop it!"

And then Grandpa's there. He hurries forward and puts his hands around Hannah's waist, steadying her, stopping her from falling.

"Come on," he says. "Come on now. Come on."

"Look!" Grandma waves her hand at the ruin that's the kitchen. "Look what she's done!"

"I know," says Grandpa. "I know." He sounds like he's calming an animal. He looks up at Hannah, still balanced on the chair. Her face is white, with a red mark where Grandma slapped her. "Hannah, go to your room," he says.

Hannah doesn't move. "She hit me," she says. "She *hit* me!"

"I know," says Grandpa. He holds out his hand. "Come on, now. Come on. There you go. We'll talk about this later."

He pushes Hannah toward the door and Hannah goes, her eyes still bewildered, like she can't believe it.

I'm still standing in the doorway. I expect Grandpa to say something to me, to ask if I'm all right, if I had anything to do with the mess, but he doesn't. He goes over to Grandma and puts his arms around her.

Grandma is almost crying.

"I can't do this," she's saying. "I can't. Don't ask me to, because I can't."

Grandpa tries to hold her but she beats her hands against his chest, face red.

"Don't touch me," she says. "Don't! I can't!"

I want Grandpa to look at me. I want not to be forgotten. But this isn't my house: It's Grandma and Grandpa's, and Grandpa is running his hands down Grandma's arms — I wouldn't dare touch her, she's so hot and furious — saying, "I know. I know, love," and suddenly I get scared. I'm not wanted here. I go and sit on the stairs and wish as hard as I can for magic wardrobes or fairy godmothers or just to be invisible and as far away from here as it's possible to be.

In the kitchen, I can hear Grandma loud and Grandpa quiet. Grandpa says, "If that's what you want to do," and Grandma says, "Someone has to." Then she scrapes her chair back and stands up. She's talking on the phone, I can hear her talking but not what she's saying or who she's saying it to. And I wonder if we're going to be sent to Auntie Meg's or Auntie Rose's, and if I'm going to have to share a room with horrible grown-up boy cousins or messy baby ones, and if I'm going to spend my whole life living in the corner of someone else's family.

I don't want to go up to my room — I want Grandpa to find me and see how sorry and miserable I am. I hear pans clatter next door and the rain still battering against the windows, and then the radio starts playing *The Archers* music and I feel tears pricking at the back of my eyes. They're making tea without me.

It's Grandma who finds me in the end. She comes through into the hall with her hands full of newspaper and broken glass and sees me.

"Molly Alice!" she says. "Whatever are you doing up here?"

"I don't know," I say miserably.

"There's no use sitting there feeling sorry for yourself," says Grandma. "Come on. Get up. You'll catch cold if you sit up there."

My mum would never say anything like that if she found me on the stairs in the dark. My mum used to get angry — she tipped a whole bowl of spaghetti over Hannah's head once — but she always said sorry afterward and then you'd eat ice cream or something to show you still loved each other. And you'd *talk* about things: what you'd done, what she'd done, what you were both going to do next time. Mum liked talking. She would never leave me sitting on the stairs all night. Neither would my dad. Probably. I feel tears rise in my eyes, and I turn my face away so she won't think I'm feeling sorry for myself again. But at the same time I *want* her to see them. So she knows how bad she's made me feel.

"Come on," says Grandma. "Come on, now. Get up. Get up, Molly," and I clench my lips, but the tears are running out of my eyes and down my cheeks and there's nothing I can do to stop them.

"Oh . . ." says Grandma. "Oh, love. None of that. Hey. Grandma's sorry. Come on. Come on, love."

She hustles me into the kitchen and sits me on a chair. Grandpa looks up from his chopping board.

"Molly? Are you all right?"

No, I want to say, can't you see? But Grandma doesn't let me answer.

"She's just tired," says Grandma. "It's not nice hearing Grandma and Grandpa shouting, is it?"

I rub my eyes. Just because I'm crying doesn't mean I like being treated like I'm five years old. Grandpa looks at me worriedly, but doesn't say anything. He carries on chopping potatoes. Grandma makes me a cup of tea in a baby mug with rabbits on it. I wrap my hands around it and watch Grandpa kitchening about and Grandma wiping her hands on a bit of cloth.

"I've been talking to your dad," she says abruptly. I jerk my head up and nearly drop my tea over my skirt.

"Are we going back home?"

"He's going to have you for the weekend," says Grandma. "And see how you all get on."

"This weekend?" I say. There's a dull ache in the bottom of my stomach. I ought to be glad, I know I ought. But all I can remember is what it was like last time we were there. I remember the way Dad used to stare at us, like he'd forgotten who we were. How Hannah used to push and push and push him until he turned into someone I barely knew, someone who could just switch off the part of him that loves us. And this time there won't be any Auntie Rose. There'll only be us.

I'm frightened, I realize.

"Aren't you pleased?" says Grandpa. He looks very like Dad suddenly. I'd never noticed it before. Like Dad, except he's not so lopsided and his skin is looser and paler; you can see it hanging off the bones under his skin. He's pale all over, Grandpa: white, wispy hair, light, watery eyes, like life has washed through him and washed him half away. I wonder suddenly if the same thing could happen to my dad. Sweep right through him and take him away from us forever.

Yes. It could.

"A whole weekend with your dad!" Grandpa says.

I clench my lips together and nod.

A whole weekend with Dad.

It's what I want, more than anything.

I nod my head up and down, trying not to cry.

25

Solstices and Equinoxes

Halloween comes. At school, we do a wall display. A witch with stripy orange-and-black tights, a vampire in a purple bow tie, and a mummy made from toilet paper stolen from the cleaning cupboard.

"If the cleaners ask, it was nothing to do with me," says Miss Shelley, and Mrs. Angus shakes her head and pretends not to see.

We make pumpkin-lanterns, with jagged mouths and slanted eyes. Miss Shelley shuts the curtains and lines them all up on the windowsill. They look wonderfully creepy.

"In medieval times," she says, "they used to carve turnips, not pumpkins. To keep evil spirits away."

"Did they have them always," says Alexander, being intelligent again, "or just at Halloween?"

"Just Halloween," says Miss Shelley. "People believed that on certain nights of the year, the barriers between worlds were weakened. Other — things — could come through."

"Cool," says Josh. "Let's call them up!" But Mrs. Angus says we have to wait till secondary school for that sort of thing.

"What kind of things used to come?" says Matthew.

"Oh, ghosts and spirits," says Miss Shelley. "Your wild hunt, Molly. Halloween was one of the nights they used to ride."

"When else?" I say. "When else are they going to come?"

Miss Shelley pushes her fair hair back behind her ears. In the half-light, she looks very much like my mum. "Solstices and equinoxes," she says. "The longest and the shortest days of the year. And the days when day and night are of equal length. September the twenty-second was the autumn equinox. The nights keep getting longer and darker now until the winter solstice."

In the dark classroom, with the curtains drawn and the pumpkin lanterns glowing, even the boys are quiet. I shiver. September the twenty-second. Was that when the huntsmen came before? Are they coming tonight?

When Grandpa suggests we might want to go trick-or-treating, Hannah groans.

"How old do you think I *am*?" she says.

Grandpa's face falters.

"Moll?" he says.

"I'm too old too, Grandpa," I say, even though I'm not, and neither is Hannah. At home, even kids from secondary school will put on a mask if it gets them sweets. But I'm not going out on my own if the Holly King is riding again.

Grandpa tries not to look disappointed.

26

Back Home

Friday night. Dad's supposed to be picking us up, but he's late. Hannah and I are packed and ready and sitting in the living room. Hannah's kicking her heels against the sofa. *Dud*-de-*dud*-de-*dud*-de-*dud*.

"Is he *here* yet?"

"He's coming," says Grandma. "Don't *fuss*. Why don't you put the telly on or something?"

Hannah flicks through the channels, but doesn't settle on anything. She starts turning the TV on and off, on and off, so the *Neighbours* characters appear and disappear, here, gone, here, gone, here —

"Stop it," says Grandma. "Hannah!" But Hannah jumps up and runs to the window.

"Is he here?"

He isn't.

I hold my book up over my face, so close that the writing blurs and separates, words merging into each other until nothing makes sense. I know I ought to feel glad about going back to Dad, but I don't.

I don't feel anything.

When he does come, Dad's awkward. He ducks his ugly head and looks at us sideways.

"Hey there," he says. "You ready?"

I nod and Hannah says, "We've been ready for *hours*," not at all like she's pleased to see him.

We're quiet in the car too. Dad says, "I hear you've been causing trouble," and gives his snorty, nervous laugh.

Hannah says, "*No*," which is totally ridiculous, as Grandma's already told Dad exactly what happened.

I say, "*I* haven't done anything. Hannah broke half of Grandpa's kitchen, and we had to have sausages out of breakfast bowls."

"Grandma hit me," says Hannah.

"It sounds like you deserved it," says Dad.

"She *hit* me," says Hannah.

"It was more like a slap," I say.

I know what Hannah's thinking. I can see it in her face. She's thinking: Mum would be furious about this. Mum's good at being furious, in a way that Dad isn't.

"What do you want me to do about it?" he says. He gives his nervous laugh again. "You live with Grandma now. If you're going to break her possessions, she's got every right to punish you."

"She hasn't got the right to *hit* me," says Hannah. "*And she's making me pay for everything.* You're our dad! Can't you stop her?"

Dad's eyes are on the tractor in front of him. "No," he says wearily. "It's none of my business anymore."

Hannah and I are speechless. I want to hit *him*.

"If it's none of your business," says Hannah, at last, "why are you having us home for the weekend?"

For the longest time, I think Dad isn't going to answer. Then he says, without looking at us, "Because your grandma asked me to."

Our house doesn't look like home anymore.

There's a stale smell that I don't remember. Like old socks, or bedrooms without air in them. There are moldy mugs and things on the table and, on the floor by the sofa, old plates with the ends of pizzas and baked-bean juice still stuck to them. There's a pile of letters and papers and bits of stuff on the hall table. The kitchen bin is full so high that when you press the lid, it doesn't open. Dad's obviously given up on opening it, but he hasn't emptied the bin. There's a plastic bag hanging from one of the cupboards, with rubbish in it.

"What's happened to the house?" says Hannah.

Dad doesn't answer.

My room is a mess too, but that's how I left it.

Someone — Auntie Rose maybe — has washed all the dirty clothes, but the rest of my stuff they've just piled on my desk. Already it feels like someone else's room. I take Humphrey out of my bag and put him on the bed, not for comfort, but just to have something that feels like it still belongs to me. It's not until I go over to the bookcase that I feel like this place is mine. My books! *Tracy Beaker* and my big old *Winnie-the-Pooh*! I want to take them all out and read them again. I wonder how many Dad will let me take back to Grandma's.

I don't think we're going to move back here anymore.

"Molly. *Molly!*"

Hannah's leaning against the door frame.

"What?"

"He didn't even tidy up for us. There's all this stuff in the fridge growing mold and things."

Probably, we ought to clean it up for him. Probably, that's part of the whole looking-after-your-parents thing those kids on *Blue Peter* do. Probably, we have to tidy everything up for Dad if we ever want to come back.

"Do you want to tidy up?" I say.

Hannah makes a snorting noise in the back of her throat.

"I want tea," she says. "Come on."

Dad's sitting in front of the television. He doesn't seem to notice the mess. He's watching the cricket match.

"Dad. Dad. *Dad!*"

"What?"

"Is there any food?"

Dad rubs his eyes.

"We could have chips, I suppose. Or there's eggs, I think. . . ."

We trail after him into the kitchen. No way would my dad let the house get like this normally. Normally, he's way tidier than my mum; he's the one who tells her off for leaving books lying around with their spines open, or stamping muddy footprints up the stairs, or bringing home pebbles and shells from the beach, then dumping them on a pile on the hall table and forgetting about them.

"Do we really need any *more* clutter?" he'd say, holding up the mess of seaweed.

And Mum would say, "Oh, the girls were going to make a picture!" Or, "We got that bit of rock on that walk in Dorset — do you remember? You can't throw that away!"

And Dad would pretend to be cross and say, "How am I supposed to remember? It's exactly the same as all the other bits of rock! If we go on like this we'll end up living in a beach hut!"

And Mum and I would say, "Let's!" at exactly the same time.

There are shells and ammonites and bits of sea-smoothed glass still sitting on the kitchen windowsill, but a spider has made a web across them. Dad opens the fridge door and stares into it like it's got a roast dinner hiding in the back. (It hasn't.) There are things decaying at the bottom of the salad drawer and a pepper all covered in mold. It smells awful too.

"Why don't you throw things out?" says Hannah.

"I'm sorry?"

"Like that. That horrible pepper with stuff growing on it. Why's it still there?"

"Oh . . ." Dad picks up the pepper and pushes at the bin lid. The flappy bit doesn't flap. He looks at the pepper for a moment, then puts it back in the fridge again.

"How about pizza?" he says.

I don't say anything.

Hannah's all excited about pizza. She bobs up and down, wanting garlic bread and chicken wings and Coke, and can she ring the pizza place?

"And strawberry Häagen-Dazs," she says to the man on the phone. Dad opens his mouth to argue, then shuts it again. He looks too tired to complain.

"I ordered ice cream," says Hannah. "Did you hear me?"

"I heard you," says Dad. "Did they say how long it's going to be?"

In *What Katy Did*, Katy runs a whole house on her own. She'd at least tidy. I wander back into the kitchen and pick up the pizza crusts off the plate. I try and squeeze them into the plastic bag hanging off the cupboard. The bag falls off, spilling bits of food onto the floor.

Dad appears in the doorway.

"What are you doing?"

"Nothing. The bin fell off the cupboard."

Dad rubs his face.

"I thought you were doing a Hannah on me," he says. "Come on, love, leave it alone. Pizza'll be here soon."

I trail after him. I bet Katy never had this problem.

In the living room, Hannah's watching *The Simpsons* with her feet up on the table. I sit on the edge of my chair. If Mum was here, we wouldn't be waiting for pizza and watching telly. We'd be doing proper family things.

"Dad," I say.

He doesn't look up.

"*Dad*. Can we play Monopoly?"

Hannah sits up.

"Yeah!" she says. "Can we? Can I be the banker? Can I be the dog?"

"No," says Dad. He doesn't stop looking at the television. He doesn't even *like The Simpsons*.

"Awww," says Hannah. "Why not?"

"Because the pizza will be here soon."

"Can we play Cheat?" I say.

"No."

"After tea?"

"No."

I stick my fingers in the hole in the chair. I know it's the wrong thing to say, but everything's wrong.

"Mum would've let us."

Hannah gasps. Dad doesn't move. He carries on staring at the telly like he hasn't heard me.

"Mum would've played Monopoly. And she would've cooked us a proper tea. You don't even have anything for breakfast! Mum wouldn't just have *sat* there —"

"Your mum's dead," says Dad.

"I *know* she's dead! Do you think I don't know that? But she would at least have been *nice* to us! She would at least have *looked* at us! She wouldn't have just *sat* there!" I'm crying now, messy, gulpy tears. "I wish *you* were dead," I say. "And Mum was alive. Mum would never have *left* us."

Dad stands up, so abruptly that I think he's going to hit me, my lovely dad is going to hit me.

"This is ridiculous," he says.

I stop mid-gulp.

"I don't know what your grandma thinks she's doing," he says. "I don't know what you think you're doing. Pretending you can come back and live here."

Hannah tenses.

"Aren't we going to?" I say.

"No."

Time stops.

"I'm sorry I'm not dead," says my dad. "If I was, maybe this whole mess would sort itself out."

This is too scary to cry about. Dad isn't crying either, but his face is moving under his skin.

"I'm phoning your grandma," he says, and he strides out of the room, pushing past me like Hannah does.

The doorbell rings.

Hannah's glaring at me.

"Thanks a lot," she says. "For ruining everything!" And she runs out of the room after Dad.

The doorbell rings again.

It's the pizza man.

"You ordered pizza?" he says.

I don't answer. I'm crying too hard.

"Can you go and get your mum or dad for me?" he says. "Only someone needs to pay."

Dad is on the computer upstairs. His eyes are open and he's staring at the screen, but his hands aren't moving.

"Dad," I say. "Dad. We need money for the pizza."

He doesn't move. I can see the bulge in his pocket where his wallet is, but I don't dare go and get it.

"Dad," I say. "The pizza's here. *Dad*."

I come a little closer and I see that he's crying.

On Saturday morning, Grandpa plays fourteen games of Cheat in a row with us.

It doesn't help.

27

Orphaned

If you only have one parent, like Hannah and I do, because our mum is dead, then you're an orphan. I always thought it was if both your parents were dead, but it's one or more.

It sounds very grand to be an orphan, like Harry Potter, or Mary in *The Secret Garden*. Hannah and I ought to be living in a children's home like Tracy Beaker does, or on a street corner, with boots with holes in them and nothing to eat. But being orphaned isn't like that at all.

Being orphaned sounds very dramatic, but it isn't really. You get used to it. You get used to anything. You get used to living in someone else's house and not having any of your own stuff or your own friends or your dad, and going to a weird tiny school where no one talks to you and Josh and Matthew laugh at you all the time. You get used to Hannah and Grandma always fighting, and Dad always going away, and not knowing whether you're going to live here forever, or if you're going home tomorrow.

You can even get used to having a hole in your life where someone used to live. A hole where you thought they'd live for always, except that one day they just step sideways, without looking back or saying good-bye, and vanish forever.

28

November

Grandpa brings us back from Dad's. All the way back, I expect Grandma to be angry with us and I think Grandpa does too, because he says, "It wasn't their fault, Edie," almost as soon as we come through the door.

Grandma runs her hand through her hair.

"I'm sure it wasn't," she says grimly. Then she sees Hannah's face. "Oh, come on, miss," she says. "Looks like we've got you for a while longer. Let's see if we can keep the new kitchen set in one piece, eh?"

But Hannah doesn't smash anything else.

It's November now and the nights are drawing in. Every day it's getting darker. If my man's right, that means the Holly King's getting stronger. Since we came back from Dad's, everything has been heavier and duller. Even the sky is heavy — gray clouds, with gray sky behind them.

Dad only comes to visit us twice in all of November.

He doesn't stay in the house long — I think he's frightened of what Grandma might say to him. They've hardly spoken since our weekend at home. He doesn't take us anywhere interesting instead, though. We go and have fish and chips by the sea in Alnmouth once and we go for a walk round the village the other time — the same boring walk we always do when we come to Grandma and Grandpa's.

Hannah doesn't fight and she doesn't break anything, but she droops. When Dad talks to her, she pulls away. Twice, when we're out together, she starts crying for no reason at all.

I don't cry. I haven't forgiven Dad either, but I can't say so. Not after what happened last time, I can't. Dads are supposed to love you whatever you do, but maybe that bit of Dad has broken, if he can send us back here after one fight. What if one day we fight and he just runs to our house in Newcastle and never comes back home?

I start to dream about the Holly King. He's snuffling round the house at night. He's bringing the winter. He sends icicles down the chimney and frost creeping up the walls of the house. He blows through the cracks in the doors and taps on the glass of my window. He's trying to get in.

I read a lot. I finish all the Secret Seven books and start on a series about mysteries. Grandma complains about how much it's costing her to order them all for me and aren't there enough books in the library already? But I've read all the Enid Blytons and Jacqueline Wilsons in Hexham Library, so what am I supposed to do? I help Grandpa in the shop.

I get very slightly taller.

December comes.

29

Mistletoe and Crime

Christmas cards have started appearing through the door. Hannah and I write one for everyone in school.

"What about Dad?" I say.

"Dads don't get Christmas cards," Hannah says. She's writing furiously, leaning over the table with her head bent over her card. I look over her shoulder.

Dear Josh,
I hope you have an utterly wretched
Christmas. I hope you don't get
anything except I know you will,
you will get a LUMP OF COAL
from Father Christmas, which will
make you CRY, because you
still believe in Santa. Sorry, Josh,
he isn't real.

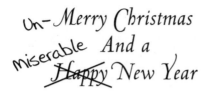

Un-~Merry Christmas
miserable And a
~~Happy~~ New Year

Lots of hate,
Hannah

"You're not sending that!" I say.

"Of course I am," says Hannah. She puts the card in the envelope, licks it, and writes SWAMP on the back.

"Sealed With A Mashed Pea," she explains. She looks at the card thoughtfully. "Or Mashed Poo, perhaps . . ."

"Dad," I say. "Can we send one to Dad? He sends Grandpa and Grandma one."

Hannah scowls at me across the table.

"Grandma and Grandpa and Dad don't live with each other," she says. "Yes? And we ought to live with Dad, only we don't. And we don't want Dad to think that's OK, so we won't send him Christmas cards, because not sending Christmas cards is what you do to people you're supposed to live with. OK?"

"OK," I say.

Hannah nods.

"Right," she says, and starts drawing little poos over the back of her envelope.

I half-expect Dad to send us a Christmas card, but he doesn't even send one to Grandpa and Grandma.

Who knows what that means?

You'd think Josh would be angry when he got a card like Hannah's, but he just laughs.

"Read mine," he says.

We all gather round Hannah as she reads it.

DEAR HANNAH THE SPANNER,

CHRISTMAS TIME, MISTLETOE AND CRIME,
JOSH IS SINGING DIRTY OLD RHYMES.
HANNAH'S ON THE FIRE,
HER GRANDMA'S ON THE TREE,
HER DAD'S HAVING A PASH WITH A GIRL FROM P.3.

JOSH THE BOSS

Merry Christmas, Joyeux Noel, Fröhliche Weihnachten, Feliz Navidad
This card is sold in aid of Save the Children.

I get a funny feeling in my stomach as I read the card.

"What's page three?" I say.

"It comes after page two," says Matthew. He laughs.

"Creep," says Hannah. "It's in *The Sun*. It's got naked girls on it."

Hannah doesn't get angry about her card either. She reads it again and smiles. Then she puts it in her pencil case.

I wonder if I'll ever understand my sister.

Christmas coming brings more things to worry about. I ask Grandpa, "We will have stockings, won't we?"

"'Course you will," says Grandpa. He's unpacking a big box of tins. "Put those on the shelf, will you, love? I'll tell Father Christmas specially."

I squash the tins onto the shelf, then come back to the counter. There's a sticker on the till with some useless barcode on it. I pick at it, trying to get it off without leaving marks on the plastic. I know Father Christmas isn't real. I know it's your mum really.

"Dad's got our stockings, though."

"He can bring them."

I keep pulling at the sticker.

"He *is* coming for Christmas, isn't he?"

Grandma's balanced on top of a stepladder, pinning Christmas things to the top of the shelves. She looks round, arms full of tinsel.

"Molly Alice," she says. "For pity's sake! Of course he's coming. Where else would he go?"

But I still worry.

We have a real Christmas tree, from Emily's parents' farm. There are piles of presents already under it — loads more than usual.

"Sympathy presents," says Hannah. "Try and look sadder next time someone comes round to visit and we might get some more."

We have more people to buy for this year too. We have another trip to Hexham with Auntie Meg. I get:

Grandma — posh chutney and a fridge magnet with *Grandmothers Are Perfect* on it, in the hope she takes the hint.

Grandpa — a bow tie with purple polka dots to make him laugh.

Hannah — a punching bag to beat up instead of me or Josh.

Dad — a photo frame with last year's school photo in it, so he doesn't forget who we are.

We get a witch doll with stripy tights for Miss Shelley and a box of chocolates for Mrs. Angus because, Hannah says, "If you give grown-ups sweets, they have to offer them round. So not those — I don't like fudge. Get those."

I have loads of pocket money saved because there's nothing to buy here except sweets, and Grandpa gives us those for free. I buy a woolly hat and box of chocolate Santas for my man — just in case.

30

Pictures in the Earth

I'm turning the Yale lock on the back door as slowly and quietly as I dare. Grandma's in the shop, and she's got sharp ears. I'm not allowed out on my own after dark, which means I'm not allowed out at all in the evenings now.

I pull the door open, quietly, quietly. Someone laughs in the shop and I slide out under their noise, pulling the door shut behind me. Free!

I've got a torch, and the spare key in my pocket. And I'm not going far. I just want to leave my Christmas presents for my man — just in case he came back.

The moon is out over the hills, pale and thin, with a huge, frosty ring. The sky is a deep, dark blue. I'm not frightened. There are shimmery beginnings of frost on the grass and a sort of witchy magic in the air and sky, which fills me up with excitement. It's the sort of night me and Mum like best.

His house sits low and mysterious under the dusky sky.

Like it's hiding a secret. My heart starts beating faster. He couldn't have come back, could he? Just in time for Christmas?

No. He couldn't.

The barn is empty. The oak tree looms over the floor and out of the hole in the barn roof, branches reaching out for the open air. I go and touch it. It's cold. The wood is dry and dark.

Is it dead?

I don't know.

I put my presents down and sit on a bag of concrete. I rest my head on my knees and wrap my arms around my legs.

"I wish you'd come back," I say. "From wherever you are."

Nothing happens.

I scratch around in the earth with the sharp end of a bit of rock. I try and draw a full moon but it just looks like a circle. I make it a head and give it horns and round eyes.

It looks stupid.

I turn the horns into leaves, growing out of the head. I draw long twigs shooting out of where the person's nose would be, if he had a nose.

Above my head, the branches of the oak tree rustle.

I draw a gravestone around the person. Underneath the grave, I draw a woman with long hair. I make the hair longer until she's buried underneath it, like Sleeping Beauty.

She looks like she's been scribbled out. Or like she's buried alive.

"Can dead people come back and visit?" I say, out loud.

The oak tree shivers. The branches move in complicated welcome, or warning.

A hand reaches forward and covers mine.

"Who's dead?" he says.

31

Two Kings

Him!

It *is* him. He's half-sitting, propped up against the tree, gray shadows falling across his face.

"You've come back!"

I'm so pleased, I forget to be shy. I jump up and hug him, as well as I can with his back against the tree.

"Where've you *been*?"

He doesn't answer. I pull away.

And, for the first time, see him properly.

He looks awful. His face is much thinner than I remember, with hollows where his cheeks ought to be and dark shadows under his eyes. It's an awful grayish-white color. It's hard to tell, in the darkness, where he ends and the tree begins.

He's shivering.

"Are you all right?" I say. And then, when he doesn't answer, "What's wrong with you?"

He shudders. I touch his hand. It's icy.

He's still dressed in nothing but his strange trousers. I take off my coat and drape it over his chest. He doesn't move.

"You can't stay here," I say. I may not know much, but I do know that. I put my arms around him and try and lift him. He gasps and cries out and I let go, helpless. "You have to come back with me. You *have* to."

"No," he says. He puts his hand on my arm.

"But . . ."

There's a noise in the doorway, behind me. I turn, too quick to be frightened, and draw in my breath.

It's the Holly King.

He's standing there in the doorway. He's bigger than I remember — taller, and stronger too.

Frost shimmers on the door frame where his hand rests.

I bite my lips. Did he follow me? Did I bring him here?

Is this my fault again?

I look sideways at my man, my Oak King. He moves his hand across to mine and squeezes it gently. He's shaking with the cold, but he can still speak.

"Not yet," he says.

The Holly King doesn't answer. He turns his black eyes on to me. "You shouldn't be here," he says.

"Leave her alone," gasps my man. That's what it is, a

gasp. His hand is still shaking, over mine. "Go home," he says.

"No," I whisper.

It's quiet in the barn, except for the rasp of his breathing.

"Listen," he says, and I bend forward, trying to catch his words. "You asked me once . . ." he says. "About bringing people back from the dead —" He shudders. I grip his hand. In the darkness of the barn, his words have a sinister edge, and suddenly I'm afraid. "For you —" he says, "I can —"

"What do you mean?" I say. "What for me? What are you going to do?" Is he going to bring my mother back? How? As a zombie? A ghost? For real? Terror rises inside me sudden as water.

"What are you going to do?"

Behind me, the Holly King stirs, frost crackling on the doorway. My man stiffens. He squeezes my hand.

"Go home," he says.

I squeeze his hand. I don't know what to say. *I love you*? It sounds silly and overdramatic. *Will you be all right*? What would I do if he wasn't? Call the police? And what does he mean by "not yet"? How much longer can he last?

I lean forward and pick up my bit of sharpened rock that I was drawing with. The Oak King, the Green Man, lets go of my hand. The beast-man steps aside in the door, leaving me room to pass. I think my man looks up, but it's so dark it's hard to be sure. He's in the shadowed side of the barn: a gray ink-shape merging into the trunk of the tree; in the darkness, you can't be sure where one begins and the other ends.

I walk very slowly past the Holly King. I'm shaking. Neither he nor my man moves. I'm holding the piece of rock cold against my palm. If I threw it straight into his eyes, could it blind him? Could it kill him?

I'm close beside him in the doorway. His strong, animal smell is all around me. All I would have to do is pull back my arm and throw.

I don't throw. I keep walking out of the door and the moment's passed. I stop and drop the rock in the mud, and suddenly I'm running, a small girl running beneath the great black arc of the sky, across the old familiar fields, to home.

32

Loki

Here's a thing about gods. You might think all gods are nice — you know, maybe the god of wine gets drunk sometimes, or the god of maths is a bit boring, but they're not really *bad* or anything. It's just, you know, if you're the god of maths, then you have to talk about long division all the time. But you need all the different gods, even gods of fractions, or rain, or underwear or whatever, because otherwise there'd be no one to ask for help when you got stuck in maths. Or ran out of underwear.

Anyway. That's what you might think, but it's not true. Because there are some gods who are just evil. There's Loki, for instance, who's this Viking god who went around doing awful things for no reason at all, like killing other gods just for fun and then refusing to cry so they never got reborn. He was so evil that the other gods tied him up in a cave underground and stuck a poisonous snake over his head, so that now the snake drips poison on him all day and all night and his wife has to stand over him with a bowl, catching it. And when the bowl is full, she pours it away and then the poison from the snake drips on Loki and he shakes so much that the whole Earth shakes too, and that's where earthquakes come from.

Or so the Vikings thought.

And that proves that not all gods are nice. Some gods will kill other gods and make sure they never get reborn. Just for fun.

33

Sleeping and Waking

All night I lie just between sleeping and waking. It's the sort of night where you think you haven't slept at all, but you must have done because where else has the night gone?

The god of the hunt is banging on our door.

"Not yet!" I shout. "Not yet!"

But, "Now," he says, and he bangs down the door and the wind comes whirling in and blows everything up — all the magazines swirling in the shop, all the tins tumbling down from the shelves — and I'm hiding in the doorway, and he's standing there on his hooved feet, watching. And my mother's there, rising up from the grave, a skeleton most beloved in blue jeans and long pale strands of yellow hair.

And I'm screaming and screaming, but then Grandpa's there, so I must have been dreaming, and he's saying, "Hush. You're all right. I've got you."

And I feel his arms around me and I'm crying, and I say, "He's coming! He's coming!"

But Grandpa holds me and he rocks me, very gentle, much more gentle than Grandma, and he says, "Shush, shush," and I wonder whether if I tell him about the Holly King, he'll be able to save my man. And I wonder if I go out now, into the night, I can get to him before the Holly King does, and somehow save him. But the night is deep and dark, and the wind is whustling round the windowpanes, dying down to nothing and then whustling again, and Grandpa is rocking me, saying, "Shush, shush," just like the man in the lane, and then antlers grow out of his head and leaves grow out of his ears and nose and he towers over me as tall as the oak tree in the barn, swaying in the breeze, and my eyes are closing and I'm falling asleep, before I can do anything at all.

34

Fear

I know I ought to go back to the barn, but I don't.

I go to the Seaman's Mission Carol Service with Grandma instead, because we always go, and remember my great-grandfather, who was in the navy. I go and see my cousin Tom play an ugly sister in his school pantomime. I stay and help Grandpa hang up all the Christmas cards ready for Dad coming to stay.

I know I ought to go back, but I don't.

35

The Year Is Dying in the Night

It's the last week of school, and we're doing hardly any work. We sing Christmas carols instead (Hannah and Josh sing the rude versions) and practice for the Christmas play. We're doing a modern version of the Nativity. At home, there were never enough parts to go around and we were all stuck being extra shepherds or angels, but here everyone except Mary and Joseph has two parts. I'm an angel with cardboard wings and a hotel keeper.

"Yes," I say. "You can sleep in my garage conversion."

I wish Grandpa had a garage conversion that my man could have. He's a sort of god, like Jesus.

Hannah and Josh are Mary and Joseph. Poor baby Jesus. Josh is a plumber instead of a carpenter, because carpenters aren't modern enough.

"You can't be having a baby," he says to Hannah. "We aren't married yet!"

"That's all you know," says Hannah. "It's the Son of God, so there!"

———•———

On the last day of term we cut up old Christmas cards to make calendars. I wonder who'll get ours this year, Grandpa or Dad? I decide to give mine to whichever one Hannah doesn't give hers to, but it's sad. Our calendars are always stuck up next to each other on the fridge in our old kitchen. I look across at Hannah to see if she's sad too, but she's busy drawing horns and a tail on a Christmas-card Joseph and doesn't seem to mind.

It's very cold at lunch. There's ice by the wall, where the shadows are. The boys start sliding on it and soon we all are, even Emily. Hannah and Josh try to push each other over. After I've nearly got knocked down twice, I go and slide on the frost, as far away from them as I can get.

All of a sudden, I have this memory of the time when I was off school because I had to go to the dentist. Me and Mum were going back to the car when we saw this ice rink, an outdoor one in the middle of town.

"Let's go skating," said Mum, and we went. And at first I just hung on to the edge and didn't know what to do, but then Mum held my hand and pulled me and we went round and round and faster and faster until we were both hot and laughing and I'd forgotten to be scared.

And after I've remembered that, I don't want to slide anymore. I go and crouch down in the cold by the school wall and watch the others.

I wonder if my man is dead yet.

Then Matthew drops icicles down the back of my coat.

And I feel like I'm going to cry, which isn't how you're supposed to feel when it's the last day of term and only four days until Christmas.

The afternoon is better. We do our play and all the parents come and watch. Actually that's only nine people and Grandpa and Grandma and Miss Shelley and Mrs. Angus, but one of the nine is Dad, so I don't mind. He comes in with Grandpa and Grandma and as soon as I see his lopsided face my whole body lets out the breath that I didn't even realize it was holding and I get the same jolt of surprise that I always get when I see him — that he looks the same as always, that he hasn't stepped further away from us in the time since I saw him last. And they all say they like the play and laugh in the right places and there is tea and coffee and juice and mince pies afterward.

The entertainment is supposed to be over with the play, but Miss Shelley starts talking to Dad about us. She tells Dad all about the Viking poems we wrote for our topic. So then Hannah has to get up and read one of hers out.

"*Vikings*
by Hannah Brooke

Vikings,
Had likings,
For pikings,
And hikings,
To places,
And races,
And chases,
Of a nun,
Without a gun,
For fun,
They wrote sagas,
And drank lagers,
And said, 'Yah! Grr!'s.
Just like you.

I would not be blue,
If I were a Viking too."

Then Josh and Matthew do kickboxing. And Alexander plays "The Snowman" on the school piano. He doesn't want to, but his mum makes him. And Emily does a ballet dance, because she goes to ballet classes.

You'd think Sascha and Oliver would be too small to do anything, but they get up and sing baby songs with Mrs. Angus, and Sascha tells this long, twisty story about a fairy that goes on forever and ever. So that's just me left.

Mrs. Angus says, "Why don't you show your dad some of your pictures?" But pictures aren't a talent show sort of thing. They're a let's-give-Molly-something-to-do-so-she-doesn't-feel-left-out thing and I don't want to do it.

I go and stand in front of everyone. I hold my hands behind my back and I turn out my feet like Emily did when she was dancing, and I say,

"Ring Out, Wild Bells

Ring out, wild bells, to the wild sky,
The flying cloud, the frosty light;
The year is dying in the night:
Ring out, wild bells, and let him die.

Ring out the old, ring in the new,
Ring, happy bells, across the snow:
The year is going, let him go:
Ring out the false, ring in the true.

Ring out the grief that saps the mind,
For those that here we see no more,
Ring out the feud of rich and poor,
Ring in redress to all mankind."

Which is a poem by Lord Alfred Tennyson, which Mum taught me for Christmas last year. When I'm done nobody claps like they did the others. Everyone's quiet for the longest time. I go back and sit by Dad and he puts his arm around me, so I must have done all right. And then Mrs. Angus goes over to the piano and we all sing carols.

We sing "I Saw Three Ships" and "Away in a Manger" and one about wassailing, which is an old word for carol-singing.

Miss Shelley says, "Any requests?"

And Emily says, "Oh, please, 'The Holly and the Ivy,'" so we sing that one.

Oh, the rising of the sun,
And the running of the deer,
The playing of the merry organ,
Sweet singing in the choir.

When we go outside it's dark and all these tiny flakes of snow are falling out of the sky, like something in a picture book, and it's so beautiful that it makes me want to cry. Everyone goes back to their cars, calling, "Merry Christmas! Merry Christmas!" and I hold on to Grandpa's hand so he doesn't slip on the ice, and I wish it could be Christmas forever.

36

Ice

But when we get home, I remember the man in the barn, and once I've remembered, I can't get him out of my head. I look out of the window at the snow falling and I think about how half of his roof has fallen in — the snow must be blowing through and right onto where he's lying.

You could freeze to death on a night like this. Even a god could.

Dad's downstairs in the kitchen with Grandma, drinking tea. I go up to the door and almost inside, but then I stop. I don't think they'll go out for a man they don't believe in on a night like this.

I go back up to the living room. Hannah's watching *Neighbours* with her hand in a box of Turkish Delight.

"Hannah."

"What?" And when I don't say anything, *"What?"*

"My man. In the barn."

"Oh, gawd." Hannah flings herself back onto the sofa and closes her eyes. "What about him?" she says dramatically, head tossed back.

"It's snowing."

"Maybe the fairies can knit him a blanket."

I twist the hem of my sweater round and round.

"Please, Hannah."

"Please *what*?"

"Come with me. Make sure he's all right."

"Molly." Hannah puts on her grown-up voice. "Imaginary people don't get cold, you know."

She turns back to the television.

"He's not imaginary!" She doesn't move. "He could *die*."

She turns up the volume. I grab the remote control. She squeals.

"*Molly!* Pack it in!"

"You're just scared," I say. "You're scared, because if you come you'll see he's real and then you'll be wrong, and you don't want to go out in the dark on your own, and you're scared of seeing a dead body, which is what he *will* be, and —"

"You are seriously weird," says Hannah. "I think you should know this." She gives this big theatrical sigh and gets up. "If he's not in his house, we're not going looking for him, OK?"

"OK."

I follow her downstairs. She barges through the kitchen door.

"Me and Moll are playing in the snow," she says. "Where's the torch?"

"Oh —" says Dad. "Well —" You can see him not wanting us to go out in the dark and not wanting to stop us playing together. "It's —" He stops. "Don't go far, will you?"

"Course not," says Hannah. She gives him her best look of withering scorn.

It's very cold. I stick my hands in my pockets and edge closer to Hannah.

"This way?" she says. She switches on the torch and it sends a fuzzy beam of light about a meter forward.

"This way."

"Come on, then."

The snow is still falling. Now it's started to settle on the ground. I imagine it settling over my man and I shiver.

The night feels strange. The trees are rustling, making noises. Like voices, whispering. I move closer to Hannah and bump into her.

"Ow!"

"Sorry."

"Where are we supposed to turn?"

"There's a gate in the hedge."

"Where?"

"It's here somewhere — there!"

I grab Hannah's hand and swing the torch round. Hannah makes this little exasperated noise and stamps off toward it. I run after her.

"How do you get it open?"

"You climb over. Hannah — the trees —"

"Ow! It's got snow on it. I can't *see* anything."

Behind me, I hear something that sounds like laughing.

"Hannah —"

"Come *on*."

The gate is already covered in snow and it's icy. I slip coming down and land in the frozen mud. It hurts.

Hannah's already ahead of me, a dark shape behind the light of the torch.

"What's that?" She sounds frightened. Hannah never gets frightened.

"What?"

"There — there's something there."

"It's his house. Remember?"

It's very dark in the barn. Snow has settled on the ground and on the black shape of the tree and on the sacks in the corner.

There's no one there.

"Happy?" says Hannah. "Can we go now?"

Snow is spattering on the roof. It blows against my back.

"Hello," I whisper.

Nobody answers.

"He's probably at a party with the fairies," says Hannah. "Come *on*."

I go to his end of the barn. It's pitchy-black. I bump against something lying on the ground.

"Moll?"

I kneel down. He's lying on his back. There's snow all over his legs and his stomach. His eyes are closed. He's shivering so hard that I can actually hear his teeth chattering.

I touch his arm. It's as cold as ice.

"Hannah," I say quietly.

And then she sees him.

For a long, long moment she doesn't say anything. Then she goes mad.

"You stupid, *stupid* little girl."

I stare.

"Why didn't you *tell* anyone he was here? He could have *died*! Why didn't you call an *ambulance* or something?"

"I did! I told you! I told Dad and Grandpa —"

"You didn't tell us he was *real*."

She runs out of the barn. I run after her.

"Where are you going?"

"Where do you think I'm going?"

"Don't leave me here!"

"Do you think," says Hannah, "I care about you?"

She runs forward through the snow and frozen grass. I follow after, as best as I can.

Everyone's in the kitchen when we burst through the door.

"There's a man in the snow," says Hannah.

Grandpa half-stands up. "In the snow? Is he hurt?"

"I don't know," says Hannah. Now we're inside she isn't angry anymore. She starts to shake.

"He's alive," I say. I run over to Dad and tug on his hand. "We need to go and rescue him."

"Where is he?" says Grandma. "Slow down and tell us properly, Moll."

"Should we call an ambulance?" says Dad.

"Have you girls still got the torch?" says Grandpa.

"It's Molly's man," says Hannah.

Everyone stops talking.

"Molly's man?" says Grandma.

"He was there all along," says Hannah.

"Molly? You were talking to a real person?"

"Of course I was," I say. "I *told* you."

"Hang on," says Dad. "What — who are you talking

about? The invisible man who makes flowers grow? He's *real*? You've been visiting a real man in the woods?" He looks at Grandma. "And you've been *letting* her?"

I pull on his hand. Clearly we're suddenly Dad's responsibility again, but I haven't got time to work out what that means. Something's changed, I know it has. Nobody could see him before. So how come they can now?

"Hurry *up*," I say. "Come and see."

37

Storm

We all go. Grandpa and Dad and Hannah and me.

The night's darker now. The snow's falling thicker and the wind's begun to blow.

Dad and Grandpa didn't want me to come, but I wouldn't stay behind. Something's shaken Dad out of his don't-fight, don't-talk mode. He was angrier than I've ever seen him.

"You *don't* talk to strangers," he said. "*Never.* What part of *never* don't you understand?"

"He's not a stranger!" I said. "We're friends."

"*No*," said Dad. He slammed his hand down on the table. "Christ, Molly! Don't you know how important that is?"

I started to cry.

"Hey," said Grandpa. "Hey, Toby." He put his hand on Dad's arm. "Let's wait and see, eh? See what's there."

But Dad pulled his arm away.

"You have no right to say anything in this conversation," he said to Grandpa. "Nothing! I haven't even *begun* on what I think of you."

Once I'd started to cry, I couldn't stop.

"He's sick," I said. I wouldn't look at Dad. "He's sick and he could be dying and all you're doing is fighting."

So now here we are, walking through the snow.

The trees are making noises, like voices.

Hurry. Hurry, or it'll be too late.

I'm so frightened I can hardly breathe.

Hurry, say the trees. *Hurry.*

I have this huge, wrong feeling. There's something strange about tonight. The world doesn't quite fit on top of itself. The edges are shifting. If we don't get there soon, something terrible will happen.

Hurry, say the trees.

Dad and Grandpa are fussing with the gate. Grandpa's opening it. How odd that all that time I've been climbing over it, it was openable after all.

I run through into the field.

"Hey, Moll —" calls Grandpa, but I can't stop. I stumble through the snow to the barn.

Now.

There's a crack. Thunder. Lightning tears the sky in two. We're the center of the storm again.

I fall through the door, into the barn. Lightning flares and for a moment it shows a picture — two men, one tall and horned, standing, the other lying facedown on the ground. The standing man has his fist raised in the air. There's something unnatural about his stillness, and the way the other lies. And then the lightning's gone and the barn is empty, save for the boom of thunder around us.

I know, without the tiniest piece of doubt, that my man isn't here anymore.

I am filled with terror.

And then the storm comes.

38

Blizzard

I'm surrounded by whirling snow. Snow is above and below and around me, like fog.

Too high, you can't get over it.

"Man!" I shout. "Man! It's me! It's Molly!"

There are voices on the wind, and shapes. Black figures towering over me, then blowing away into nothing. Things with wings and eyes.

Too low, you can't get under it.

"Man!"

Too wide, you can't get round it.

"Come back!"

I know where he is.

"Please!"

I was too late.

He's dead.

It's my fault.

I'm crying now and shaking. There are dark shapes all around me, laughing in the wind. It's the horned god, the Holly King, or something worse. The things that

Miss Shelley said come through when the barriers between worlds are weakened. Ghosties and ghoulies and long-leggety beasties and things that go bump in the night.

Other voices are calling.

"Molly! Molly!"

There's ice in my lungs. I can't breathe.

"Molly! Where are you?"

There's torchlight, and shapes in the darkness.

I stumble forward, blind in the night. Things are laughing on the wind, catching at my coat and scratching my hands with grabbing fingers. The air is thin tonight.

Things are coming through.

"Molly!"

I pull away from the grabbing things and they tear at my hair. I stumble forward, but now something else is twining through my fingers. It's twigs. Tree-hands, their branches reaching down and holding me.

"Moll! Where are you?"

I am held and rocked in the arms of the trees. Dark hands reach down and touch my face. I don't move. I hardly breathe. The snow and the cold are gone. Here and now, I am safe and untouchable.

"There you are!"

The tree-arms are gone. I fall and land face forward in the snow. I'm crying and crying.

"Molly, my love, what's the matter?"

It's Dad. Big and dark and anxious.

I'm crying so much I can hardly see him.

"Mum!" I cry. "I want Mummy!"

"Moll, Molly, my love —"

His arms go around me. I twist out of them.

"I want Mum!"

"Molly-mop —"

I lean back as far as I can. I scream and kick.

"No! I want Mummy! I want Mummy!"

He lifts me up and carries me away through the night.

39

The End of the World

It's the very middle of the night. The policemen have gone. They found nothing, not even footprints in the fast-falling snow. I told Grandma they wouldn't, but she called them anyway. It's very late. Everyone's asleep except me.

Humphrey and I are in Hannah's bed. Hannah's in my bed, where Dad's supposed to be, and Dad's on my mattress on the floor. That was Grandma's idea.

"The child needs her dad," she said. "Clearly." And she dumped Dad's suitcase at his feet. Dad didn't argue. He sat with his arms around me, chin resting against my head, holding me so tightly I could feel the rim of his watch digging into my side.

Everything's back-to-front and topsy-turvy.

Dad's asleep on the floor by my bed. He's got his back to me but I can hear him breathing.

It's dark. The only light is from the lamp on the bed-side table. There's this pool of soft, orange light, long orange-and-gray shadows on the wall and blackness out of the window.

The wind is still blowing and the snow's still falling. I think it's raining too, if you can have snow and rain at the same time.

It's like being in the middle of a blizzard.

It's like the end of the world.

I can't sleep. I can't stop thinking.

What if he wasn't Miss Shelley's god after all?

What if he was just a man?

Hannah said I should have done something. Something to save him. If I was older — if I was better — if I was Mum or Dad or Hannah or Grandpa —

If I was any one of those people, I would have done something.

If I was anyone but me, I would have saved him.

He didn't have anyone else.

He had me, and I did nothing.

40

Inside Outside

I lie on my back and stare at the ceiling.

I can hear noises against the window. Snow hitting the glass, wet and heavy.

"Mum," I whisper, but she isn't here. I know she isn't, but if I close my eyes I can almost imagine that she's close — in the next room, maybe, or on the floor beside Dad. Tonight, everything is so strange. Perhaps if I say exactly the right words or do exactly the right thing at the right time, she'll come back.

I climb out of bed, taking the horrible old-fashioned quilt and wrapping it round my shoulders. The stairs make noises as I creak down them — *creak, creak, creeeak*. I feel for the walls with my hands, so I don't fall.

The kitchen tiles are cold, even through my socks. I go to the back door and look out the window. All I can see is black and whirling snow, forever.

"Moll?"

It's Hannah. Her face is red and white in the darkness.

"What are you doing?"

She comes over to where I'm standing.

"Watching."

It's very dark in the garden. The trees are moving in the wind; you can hear them creaking.

Tonight is the longest night of the year. Absolute midwinter.

"Moll," says Hannah. "It's cold. Come back upstairs."

But there *is* something different about tonight. The Green Man is gone and that changes everything.

"Let's go," says Hannah. "Come on."

I don't move.

"What was that?" Her voice is high and frightened. *"Molly!"*

I can hear it too.

There's something there.

There's a new sound; not the snow, not the wind, something else, sort of whispery. And light too — not torchlight, fainter. What is it? Is it —

"*Moll*," says Hannah. "There's something coming!" She tugs on my arm, but I pull away.

And see her.

She's standing in the snow, clear as anything. She

doesn't look like a ghost. She looks absolutely real. She looks so real that I wonder if we should open the door and let her in.

She stands there smiling at us, normal as anything, just smiling at us through the glass.

Then she's gone.

41

Quiet

Outside, the world is quiet. Inside, we're curled up together in my bed, cold toes pressed against cold legs, arms around each other, buried in a pile of every quilt and blanket we can find.

"Did you see her?" says Hannah, again.

"Yes," I say.

"Was it real?" says Hannah. "Was it Mum?"

"Yes," I say. "I think so."

We're quiet, thinking. Hannah moves beside me, under the quilt.

"Molly?" she says.

"Mmm?"

I'm watching the shadows of the curtains on the wall. Is a shadow something real? Is a ghost?

"Don't you mind?" says Hannah.

Does it matter?

"Mind what?" I say.

What about cold? I'm thinking. Is cold something real? Or night? You can't touch them. But they're there.

"Living here. With Grandma."

"Of course."

"You never say," says Hannah. I think about it.

"We can't go back and live with Dad," I say at last. "Even if he wanted us, we couldn't."

Hannah pulls the quilt up over herself.

"Other dads do," she says. "And mums. Mum would've, wouldn't she? He could've. If he'd really tried, he could. He just didn't want to."

I'm tired suddenly. I'm tired of Mum being gone, and Dad living away, and everything being so complicated. I'm tired of trying to understand it all. I rest my head against her shoulder.

"Is that really true?" I say.

Hannah doesn't answer for the longest, longest time.

"Hannah?"

She twists around and rubs her head against my cheek.

"No," she says. "Not really."

We're quiet.

It's the longest night of the year.

We lie together there in the bed, waiting for the day to come.

42

Dad (Almost) Talking to Me

"M oll," says my dad, kneeling on the floor beside me. "Are you listening? Moll?"

I'm sitting under a blanket in Grandpa's big chair. I'm watching *A Muppet Christmas Carol* and eating cheese on toast and tomato soup. It's like being ill, the same heavy feeling.

"Was —" He stops, then starts again. "Was there really someone in the snow?"

I nod. "My man."

"Moll . . ." Dad stops again. You can see him fighting to get whatever it is he wants to say out. "I don't think your man was that sort of real," he says eventually. "Was he? Hey? Not real like —" He looks at me like he wants me to say it for him, but I'm saying nothing. "Real like Father Christmas is real," he says eventually. "Or the Easter Bunny. Hey?"

"Real's real," I say.

"Yes," says Dad. "I know. But . . . the policemen looked last night, Moll. There wasn't anyone there. I think —"

He stops. "It's . . . like a story," he says. "It *feels* real — but it doesn't *really* happen."

"But it *did*," I say hopelessly. "It did."

I expect him to argue. Mum would have argued. Grandma would have dismissed me. Grandpa would kiss me and tell me he loved me anyway. But Dad just opens his mouth and shuts it again, like he can't think of anything to say.

43

Christmas Day

It's very, very early. It's still dark.

It's Christmas morning and the stocking on the end of my bed is full; I can see it. I want to know what's in it, but I'm scared to look. I'm scared that Dad doesn't know how Christmas stockings work, like Mum did. Does he know there's supposed to be an orange? And nuts in shells? And chocolate money and a box of chocolates? Does he know there's always a book and a soft toy?

Outside, it's stopped snowing, but there's still this thin, pale coating of snow over the roofs of the houses. It's a white Christmas. Normally, this would be the most exciting thing ever, but now it just looks empty. Like the whole world knows my man isn't there anymore. I'm scared that this emptiness will get into Christmas and spoil it.

Christmas is too important to spoil.

I pull my stocking off the bed and go into Hannah's room. She's still asleep, lying on her stomach, her face buried in the pillow. I shake her shoulder.

"Hannah. Han-nah."

She moans.

"It's Christmas."

Hannah rolls over and rubs her eyes.

"Are there presents?"

"Lots."

Hannah doesn't care about things not being right when there are presents. She tips her stocking out on the bed and starts tearing the wrapping paper off things. There's a soft toy dog, a box of chocolates, a CD ... but then I can't wait any longer.

And it's OK. I don't know if Dad bought the things himself or if Grandma or one of my aunties helped, but it's OK. All the things that ought to be there *are* there, and more — a hardback Jacqueline Wilson book (Mum only ever bought the paperbacks), a notebook with unicorns on it and unicorn stickers, a friendship bracelet kit and a DVD of *The Secret Garden* that either Auntie Rose bought by mistake or surely, surely means we're going back home soon, because Grandpa doesn't have a DVD player.

Best of all are the little pile of things at the bottom of the pillowcase that come from the UNICEF catalog, which is where Dad gets all his Christmas presents. They're the least exciting things in the whole stash — a T-shirt with a dove on it, a jigsaw puzzle, and a cookbook of different foods from around the world. Hannah barely looks at hers. But I keep mine close beside me, because I know for certain that they come from Dad.

Christmas happens.

I get presents from all sorts of random people who never normally send me things. I get some from people I never even knew existed — Great-auntie June, who's Grandpa's sister and breeds cats — Terry and Maggie, who used to be our next-door neighbors when I was a baby — someone called Linda, who even Dad has never heard of.

"Who *are* these people?" says Hannah.

"They're people who care about you," says Dad, but Hannah isn't impressed.

"Do I have to write them all thank-you letters?" she says, waving a bottle of bubble bath. "Even for stuff like *this*?"

"Next year," says Grandma, "I might not bother buying you a present, if that's how you behave."

"I liked yours," says Hannah quickly. I got Rollerblades from Grandpa and Grandma but Hannah got money, which she likes much better.

After we've opened the presents, we sit quietly together in the living room. It's dark apart from the Christmas tree, which is glowing away in a corner, little colored lights shining off the tinsel. I don't think there's anything more beautiful in the world than a Christmas tree.

Hannah's sitting on the floor rearranging her present stash again. Hannah can never sit still for long. Grandpa's leaning back in his chair watching Dad. Grandma's drinking her Christmas sherry, watching Grandpa, watching us.

These are my family, I think. I squeeze my eyes tight shut to save the picture in my head. I remember the Holly King, still out there.

Go away, I think, as loud as I can. *Don't get these. These are mine. Don't get anything else that belongs to me.*

44

You Owe Me a Bear Cub

New Year comes. Dad goes back home. Last year, I would have expected him to take us with him, but this year I wouldn't be surprised if he left without even saying good-bye.

Dad seems to care, though. The night before he goes, he teaches me and Hannah poker and stays up until after midnight playing with us for IOUs written on bits of paper. He's better at games than he is at talking about what's real and what isn't. In the end, he loses everything, leaving us both with paper scraps promising me a bear cub, a Chinese junk, and a lightsaber, and Hannah a mansion, a Mercedes, and a million pounds.

When I go to bed, he lifts me up off the ground and squeezes me.

"All right, Molly mine?" he says.

I wrap my legs around his hips and rest my head against his shoulder.

"You owe me a bear cub," I say.

"I owe you a lot more than that," he says, and he lowers me back to the floor and goes downstairs, leaving me wondering.

When I wake up in the morning, he's gone.

We go back to school. We've finished the Vikings and we're doing Bridges, which Miss Shelley says we're not to complain about because it Wasn't Her Idea and at least it'll give us something to do with all those cereal boxes.

It stays cold. Not exciting snow-and-hail cold. A dull, gray, miserable kind of cold.

I don't see the Holly King again. Maybe he won't ever come back. Now he's won.

I go back to the barn, once, before Dad leaves. I look inside and all around the back. I call him by all the names that I know. Oak King. Green Man. I don't call for long. I feel silly calling for someone who isn't there.

When I'm done, I go and look at his tree. It's quite dead. The wood is pale and chipped and worn away. It's shiny with wet and slimy with rot. It looks about five hundred years old.

Looking at it, I find it hard to remember that I believe in things that come back from the dead. I can barely believe, looking at it, that it was ever even alive.

And back in the real world, no one has noticed that everything's changed. Josh and Hannah are still Josh and

Hannah. Emily is still Emily and Dad is still Dad. He still comes and takes us out, though now he does seem to be trying to make more of an effort.

"Look," he says. "I've bought you a present." And he brings out a magazine, or a Kinder egg, or a second advent calendar cheap in the sales.

"Thank you," I say, and he puts his head on one side.

"Hey," he says. "Moll. It's not the end of the world."

I don't answer.

Grandpa is still Grandpa. When we come home from school he looks up from the till.

"How was school?" he says.

"Horrible," grumps Hannah, and stumps through to the kitchen to see if there's any past-the-sell-by-date cake to eat.

"Really horrible?" says Grandpa, and I rest my arms on the counter and lay my head down on top of them.

"OK really," I say, and he pats my shoulder.

"How about you put the new stock out for me?" he says — or mop the floor — or take those boxes out — or mind the till while I make a cup of tea? And I'll nod and do whatever it is he's saved for me, so long as I get to stay here close by him.

As I work, I'll catch him looking at me.

"Really OK?" he'll say sometimes, like I'm hiding some big terrible secret. I don't tell him that I don't need a terrible secret. The things he knows about are terrible enough.

And January turns into February, and I come up the hill from school with the wind in my hair and the cold in my fingers and I wonder if I'll feel like this forever.

45

Candlemas

Today, when we pile into the schoolroom, Miss Shelley is up by the whiteboard with a look on her face that says we aren't doing maths this morning.

"Today," she says, "is a very special day. Can anyone tell me why?"

The boys all stick their hands in the air.

"It's your birthday!"

"It's Mrs. Angus's birthday!"

"We're having a party!"

"We're having a trip!"

"We're going home!"

I don't want to go on a trip and my home is a long way from here. What I hope is happening is art. Something quiet and soothing, with flowy water or colored beads or crayons in soft pastel colors.

"No," says Miss Shelley. "Today is Candlemas."

"What's Candlemas, miss?" says Matthew.

"Candlemas is the midpoint between the winter solstice and the spring equinox," says Miss Shelley. She looks at our blank expressions (not mine! I remember this!) and laughs. "In one sense," she tells us, "it's the first day of spring. In Roman times, people used to have processions through the streets with torches and candles. They would take the candles to churches to be blessed."

"Torches?" says Matthew, like the Romans had electric torches, with batteries.

"Flaming torches, stupid," says Hannah.

Miss Shelley puts us into groups and we make candles all morning. Usually we're three groups: boys, girls, and littlies, and it ends up with me and Emily getting bossed about by Hannah. But today Miss Shelley puts Hannah with Josh and Matthew, and Alexander with me and Emily.

It's a nice change not being in a group with Hannah. I can hear her at the other table, arguing over scissors.

"But you aren't even *using* them!"

"They're *mine*!"

Emily and Alexander and I look at one another shyly.

Miss Shelley gives out cardboard to make candle molds and crumbly wax and soft white string for wicks.

Emily makes cone-shaped candles. Lots of cone-shaped candles.

Alexander's candle is like a rocket. It's the inside of a

toilet roll with a cardboard cone taped to one end of it. He makes the mold, then he stares at it for ages.

I've never talked properly to Alexander before. He always tags around with Josh and Matthew, but I think that's just because there aren't any other big boys in the school.

I like Alexander's rocket mold. And I think I like Alexander. So I say, "What's wrong?"

Alexander scratches the back of his head. Then he says, "It's fins. It needs fins. To go on the side."

We look at the candle.

"You could make them out of cardboard," says Emily, in her soft voice.

"They have to be wax," says Alexander. "A red wax candle and blue wax fins."

"You should make more molds," I say. I lean forward to show him. "Out of plasticine. Then, when the wax has set, you peel away the plasticine and stick the fins to the candle. See?"

Alexander's plasticine rocket-fin molds seem to work. Everyone else has cardboard molds except for us. Emily makes a fish-shaped plasticine mold and a dog-shaped mold. I make molds that are supposed to look like flowers, only they don't quite come out right.

It's nice. Almost like having friends.

"Look at Alexandra!" says Matthew, barging past our end of the table. "Making flowers with the girls!"

Alexander goes bright red.

"I am not!"

And he spends the rest of the lessons bent over his candle, so it doesn't look like he's talking to us.

We melt the wax and pour it into the molds and leave it to set while we do maths, then transporter bridges, then the water cycle (again). Just before home time, Miss Shelley turns off the big light and we light them all. Rocket candles and rainbow candles and candles scratched all over with graffiti.

There's a whole tableful of pointed yellow lights.

I close my eyes. Even with them shut, I can still see the fuzzy orange candle flames.

Tiny little points of light in the darkness.

46

Bonfires and Magic

When we get home, Jack's having a bonfire.

I go out to watch him. The smoke has a wonderful woodsy smell about it. The air is sharp and there's this pale blue sky, so big and empty it almost hurts, with just a few stringy clouds hovering round the edges.

"Like it?" says Jack, and I nod.

I like Jack. I like fire. I like how different things behave when you put them on it. Crisp packets burn with this big flame and then shrivel away to nothing. Planks sit there for ages making up their minds, but once they start burning they go and go. Logs crackle. Wet wood hisses and smokes. And the leaves from the hedge make friendly *pop — pop — pop*ping sounds.

"Double, double, toil and trouble," says Jack. "Fire burn and cauldron bubble. Little witch, you are."

"That's right," I say. "I'm making a spell. Double, double, double," and I walk round the fire three times widdershins, which is the opposite way to clockwise and also magic.

"Don't you cast any spells on me!" says Jack.

"I'm making a weather spell," I say. "A spell to make it spring again."

"Ah," says Jack. He pokes the fire with a bit of stick. "Spring'll come round without anyone wishing for it," he says.

"Soon?" I say.

"Soon enough," says Jack, and throws the stick on the fire.

47

Alliances Forged in Clay

At school, the candle project still isn't finished. Now we have to make clay candleholders. In the same groups as before.

Matthew groans, deeply and dramatically.

"Why can't we swap groups, miss? Why do we have to be with *her*?"

"Because," says Mrs. Angus, "it's about time you learned how to treat a lady."

Josh and Matthew think this is hilarious.

"Watch out," Josh coos to Hannah. "*You* can't have the clay. You're a *lady*. *You* might get dirty."

"Shut it, gimp," says Hannah.

Alexander and Emily and I make a big candleholder together.

"A *candelabra*," says Alexander.

He rolls the word around in his mouth like it's something magical. I like the idea of a word as magic. I give

Alexander my best words back. Nocturnal. Luminescence. Malevolence. Sprat.

Alexander of the Roman-fort-loving lecturer parents is more than up for those.

"Mulligrubs," he says.

Emily and I stare.

"That's not a word."

"It is!" says Alexander. "It means to be sad."

We're both suspicious. But Alexander hasn't stopped yet.

"Oscitate," he says. "That means yawning. Or defenestrate — that means to throw someone out of a window."

I start to laugh. "There isn't a word for throwing someone out of a window!"

"There is," says Alexander. "Defenestrate. And porknell — that means fat as a pig. And —"

"You're making these up!"

"I'm not," says Alexander. He looks hurt. "I've got a book of them at home."

We both look at Emily. She ducks her head, staring at her clay.

"Your turn," says Alexander.

Emily doesn't say anything. She turns her head away.

"It doesn't have to be a long word," I say, to help her.

"Splat!" says Alexander, to show her.

"Squish."

"Boom."

"Kablam."

Emily smiles, a small, shy smile like a pink hamster nose poking out of its house.

"Sparkle," she says.

"Shine," says Alexander.

"Fine."

"Wine, opine, dine —"

"Give it to me!"

Over on the other end of the table, Hannah and Josh are fighting again. Josh is holding the clay knife behind his back. Hannah lunges for it and he stumbles back, laughing.

"Give it!"

"*Ladies* don't need knives," says Josh. "Knives are for *boys*. A *girl* might cut herself."

Matthew gives a hiccuppy little laugh.

"I'll do your cutting," says Josh. "You show me what you want cutting, I'll do it. Just —"

Way over on the littlies' bit of the table, Sascha squeals. Mrs. Angus turns round, but she's too late to stop Hannah from picking up Josh's entire dragon candelabra (with detachable flames) and throwing it at him, splat bang in the middle of his face.

Hannah's in the biggest trouble ever.

"I started it, miss," says Josh, but Miss Shelley doesn't care.

"Hannah knew exactly what she was doing," she says. She makes Hannah write lines, like a Victorian schoolgirl.

I must not throw clay.
I must not throw clay.
I must not throw clay.

"Sorry," Josh whispers as he bumps past her. He's got clay all over his sweater, and bits of clay slicked into his hair and ears where the soaping didn't reach. He looks like a goblin. Hannah doesn't say anything, but she gives him this big, triumphant smile.

At break, Alexander goes off after Matthew and Josh, but he looks over his shoulder at me and Emily. Josh ignores him. He's making an iceball out of the dirty bits of crushed ice at the edge of the playground. When Hannah comes out, he yells, "Oi! Mudwoman!" and lobs it at her.

It hits the side of Hannah's coat. She stands utterly

still, then she charges at Josh, stuffing bits of crushed iceball down the back of his coat. Josh squirms.

"Oi! Get off me! Madwoman!"

But he's laughing, and so is Hannah. I watch, trying to figure out if they're friends now, or enemies. But I can't work it out.

48

By Moonlight

Tonight, I take my conkers down from the window-sill. They've gotten smaller and kind of shriveled, dark and hard. They remind me of the bits of wood and stone that Mum used to collect, and it makes me happy to think that I've brought a little piece of my mother into my bedroom. I sit on my windowsill with a conker in each hand and try to feel the spark of life that Miss Shelley told us about. I imagine it like a seed, buried deep under the layers of conkerness. I poke at it, trying to hurry it up.

Hurry up, I tell them, in my head. *Wake up. Grow.*

When I fall asleep, I dream.

I dream that there's someone in our garden. It's a boy, wearing nothing at all. I can see his bare back in the moonlight. He's kneeling in the snow, shivering. More than shivering. His whole body is shaking. He's kneeling there, bent over with his arms wrapped around his chest, shaking and shaking and staring and staring all around him like he's never seen frost or trees or gardens or the moon before.

I kneel up in bed and push my head out under my curtain, and I watch him. The moon is big and bright. The sky is full of stars. Frost glitters on the branches of the trees. There's absolutely nothing making any noise at all except this boy, gasping and shaking. Everything else is still.

The boy holds up his hands and stares at them. He turns them over and over in the moonlight like he's never seen hands before. He looks up to my window and I duck my head back behind the curtain so he can't see me. I'm trembling. I know exactly who he is, the way you do know things in dreams. It's my man, my green god, come back as a boy. I'm frightened, but I'm also full up with excitement. He ought to be dead and he isn't. He's come back.

I open the curtains very slightly and peer through. He's standing up, walking round the garden. He's not shaking now. He's almost exactly the same size as me. He touches the branches of the trees and they shiver under his fingers. He kneels under the tree at the bottom of the garden and he touches the grass, here and here and here.

What's he doing? I press my face up to the window to try and see, but it's too dark, it's too far away.

He's standing under the trees, looking at the grass that he's touched. Is there something there now? I can't be sure. He turns and looks up to my window again, a bare, beautiful boy in the moonlight.

Then he's gone.

49

Snowdrops

Next morning, when I take the crusts out for the birds, there are footprints in the frozen grass. They start in the middle of the lawn and they go all around the edge of the flower bed. Then they stop.

In the frost under the oak tree, where the boy was crouched last night, there are little flowers. Snowdrops.

"Well!" says Jack, smiling at me from his kitchen window. "Did you make those, little witch?"

I blink at him. I don't say anything.

"Haven't you ever seen snowdrops before?" he says.

I don't answer. I touch the flowers very gently, making sure that they're real.

50

Happiness

Coming down the hill to school, I'm singing.

"There is singing in the desert, there is laughter in the skies —"

"Shut *up*," says Hannah.

"No," I sing. "No, no. Hey — hey, Hannah? Have you ever had a dream that came real?"

"Have I *what*?"

"Have you ever dreamt something then had it come true?"

"Yes," says Hannah. "I dreamt I had a little sister who wouldn't stop singing, so I *grabbed* —" She pounces. Normally I would scream, but today I just laugh and wriggle free and run off down the road. Hannah chases after me and grabs me by my coat.

"You'll never catch me," I sing. "Never, never."

I tear free and run down the hill to school.

I can't remember the last time I laughed so much with Hannah.

All day at school, I look for signs that he might have been here. New flowers, growing where they weren't before, green spikes of grass, new leaves on the trees.

There's nothing.

As soon as I get home, I go into the garden. I look for him in all the hiding places, even silly ones where he couldn't possibly be.

I can't find him.

Over in his house, Jack sticks his head out of the window.

"Lost something?" he calls.

"Have you seen a boy?" I call back. "My size, with no clothes on?"

Jack laughs.

"Oh, aye?" he says. "Who's that — Alexander, or one of those Haltwhistles?"

"Not them," I say. "A special boy. He's magic, I think."

"I see," says Jack. "Well, if I see any magic boys with no clothes on, I'll let you know."

I go back to the barn again, but it looks the same as it has all winter.

Empty.

"Hello?" I call. "Boy? It's me — Molly."

I have no idea if he'll remember me or not. He's a whole new person now, after all.

Not that it makes any difference. He's not there.

I sit on a bag of concrete and wonder where else to look. He could be anywhere. If he's even real. Maybe I *was* dreaming.

Then I look up and see it.

His oak tree.

I can feel the happiness bubbling up again inside me. I go over and touch it; the tree I thought was dead. I reach out and touch the green place in the bark, where new wood is beginning to show through the old.

51

The Amazing Upside-Down Boy

I'm too full up with jittery excitement to go back home.

I go to the wood behind the houses, where the youth hostel is. It isn't a proper forest, like the Forbidden Forest or the wood with the lamppost in Narnia. It's not the sort of wood you'd think a god would hide in. It's full of dead wood and ivy and squelchy patches and nettles and you only have to walk for about ten minutes before you hit an edge.

But I can't think of anywhere else he might be.

"Boy?" (Very quietly.) "Boy?"

And there he is.

He's hanging upside down from a tree. He's got some trousers from somewhere — brown, leafy, Peter Pan–type trousers. Maybe he's magicked them for himself. He's wearing a wreath of ivy leaves, but it doesn't look girly. It's all mashed up in his hair, which is wilder than I remember: big, messy curls sticking out in all directions.

"This place is *great!*" he says.

He's exactly the same size as me. I think his eyes are the same color as before, but they're different. My man's eyes were gentle — this boy's look more like Josh's when he's excited about something.

"Do you remember me?" I say.

The boy screws up his eyes.

"Of course I do," he says. "You were there last night, weren't you? You were hiding, but I saw you — that's where I know you from."

I bite my lip. I'm not at all sure this counts as remembering me.

"Where did you come from?"

"Somewhere," he says. "Somewhere *you've* never been."

"You were —" I hesitate, not sure how to put it politely. "Do you remember what happened? At Christmas?"

"Of course," he says. But he looks uncertain. "Why are you asking all these questions?" he says. "Who are you, anyway?"

"I'm Molly. Molly Brooke."

He still looks puzzled.

"You look like one of the house-people, but you aren't a house-person, are you?"

"I am," I say. "But I'm your friend too."

"Everyone's my friend." He laughs at me, upside down. "Look —" He holds out his hand and a green shoot curls out from between his fingers and twists around his hand

and up his arm. "Can you do that, Molly Brooke person?" he says.

"No," I say. "No, I can't." I chew on my lip. "You do know not everyone's your friend, don't you?" I say. "You do remember about the Holly King?"

"Of course," he says airily. He flings himself forward off the branch and lands on his hands. "Look!" he says, upside down, balanced on his hands. "Can you do this?"

"Yes," I say, "I can, actually. But you have to remember about the Holly King. He tried to kill you! And he's still after you! You have to be careful —"

"Be careful, be careful," says the boy. "Who's afraid of the Holly King? I've got work to do!"

He walks toward me on his hands, then drops his feet back down to the earth. He crouches in the grass, touching it with his fingertips. Little green sprouts push their way up through the earth. Flowers appear, snowdrops, frail and white.

"Can you do *that*?" he says.

I don't answer. I'm looking at his trousers. They're made of brown planty shoot, all woven together. You can see his legs through them. They're smooth and brown and strong, but slashed across them are the marks of old scars, deep and white.

The sort of scars you'd get from the bite of a dog.

Or a wolf.

I run down the last bit of lane home. There are green shoots under the hedges where daffodils are going to come soon, and a cold blue sky above me. When I burst into the kitchen, Dad's there. He's started coming round unexpectedly since Christmas. He's drinking tea and playing thumb wars with Hannah.

"One, two, three, four, I declare thumb war. Thumb war!"

Thumb wars are a Dad thing — me and Mum are rubbish at them. Hannah's very good. She kneels up on her chair, twisting Dad's arm all the way up and round. I'm not sure if she's really that strong, or if Dad's letting her win.

"Hey, hey, love, be careful," he says. He looks up and sees me. "Hey, Moll! Where've you been?"

"Up in the woods," I say. "I saw —" I stop.

"Who'd you see?" says Hannah. Her face is red, strands of hair sticking to her forehead. "Josh?"

I hesitate. Dad's smiling. He's come all the way from Newcastle to see us.

"No one," I say. I sit down on the other side of Dad. "Just trees and stuff. Can I have a go?"

"Let's pick something we can all play," says Dad. "Cards, maybe?"

Emily on Ice

Emily's birthday is in February. She doesn't invite everyone to her party like Matthew did his. She just asks me and Alexander.

"What about us?" says Matthew.

Emily shakes her head. Her eyes get big and round.

"Don't be so rude," says Mrs. Angus. "Emily can invite who she likes. I'm not surprised she doesn't want you there, after what you do to her."

Matthew and Josh were showing Hannah kung fu yesterday. Only Josh got fed up with the whole unarmed-conflict thing and whacked Matthew over the head with Emily's chair. While Emily was trying to sit on it.

I don't say anything to Emily when I get my invitation, but I can't stop smiling, all through spellings-and-tables.

The party is a skating party.

"Have you ever been skating before?" Emily's mum asks us in the car.

"Once," I say.

Emily can skate already. She slides straight off onto the ice and spins around. She looks like a ballerina.

"Come on, you two!" Emily's mum says to Alexander and me.

Alexander looks terrified. He holds on to the side and edges his way round. Even I can do better than that. I don't hold on to the edge. I inch forward, arms held out. Emily skates round me.

"Push sideways with your feet," she says. "Like this."

I try and I go forward. Emily holds on to my hand.

"Let's go fast," she says. I'm sure I'm going to fall. I'm sure. But I push with my feet and I seem to do OK.

Emily on ice is completely different from everyday Emily. She talks, like a real person. We skate all the way around and then we pick up Alexander, who's still clinging to the side. We hold one hand each and pull him.

"Oh," he says. "I don't like it. I don't like it."

"Not even fast?"

"*Especially* not!" he says, and falls over.

He goes off with Emily's little brother to buy crisps. Emily and I go round again. Emily shows me how to go backward and I *almost* do it. And I only fall over twice the whole time.

"That's a lovely skating skirt, Molly," says Emily's mum. She can skate too. My skirt is the red one Mum made me. "It goes lovely with those dark curls."

"I hate my hair," I say. "I wish I had blond hair."

"I wish I had curls," says Emily.

Afterward we have chips in the café, and I teach Emily Mum's spy game, where you have to work out which of the people around you are secret agents in disguise. The hunched-up old lady with the wrinkles and the pink lipstick definitely is — why would someone so small and shriveled-looking want to go ice-skating?

"Unless she's an alien," says Emily, and we both go off into giggles.

"Emily, behave," says Emily's mum, but she smiles at me and Alexander. "I'm so pleased Emily's met you two. She had a hard time when she started at that school."

"School's horrible," says Alexander. I look at him, surprised. I thought Alexander liked school. I thought everyone did except me (and maybe Hannah). And actually there are lots of things at school that I like. Miss Shelley, and art, and nature, and playing games all together, and the play, and Emily and Alexander and . . .

". . . if she'd say yes?"

Emily's mum is looking at me.

"What?" I say.

"I said, you seemed to enjoy skating," she says.

"Oh yes."

"Well," says Emily's mum. "Emily comes here every Wednesday. It's a bit lonely being the only one from here.

We'd be happy to bring you along, if your grandma doesn't mind."

Emily sits straight up. "Yes!" she says. "Come, come, come!"

"And you too, of course, Alexander," Emily's mum says, but Alexander looks horrified.

"Will you?" says Emily. "Will you, will you?"

I don't say anything. I'm thinking — about having friends. About learning to spin and go properly fast. If I could be a skater when I grow up, it wouldn't matter that I don't have blond hair. Or maybe I'll be an artist, or run a shop like Grandma, or write books about all the magic in the world. Or maybe I'll do them all. I could do anything, I think, and I feel the corners of my cheeks turning up, turning into a smile so big it's like my whole face is beaming.

"Yes, please," I say.

53

A Flower for March

There are rabbits in Grandpa's garden. I can see them in the twilight as I wheel my bike back to the shed. Bright eyes, long ears, and the flash of a white tail. They're after Jack's vegetable patch.

March has come. Rain and wet grass and the first few leaves on the oak trees. The day after Emily's party, I find the first daffodils under the tree in the garden. Emily-daffodils.

Dad brings us three purple crocuses in a bowl.

"One for you. One for Hannah, and one for your grandma, for looking after you."

"What about Grandpa?" said Hannah. "Grandpa does all the work!"

Perhaps my boy in the wood made these crocuses. Is he the god of garden centers too? And if he isn't, who is? Does he really make all the flowers in the world? Or are there different summer gods in Australia and Africa and America? How far does he stretch — all of Britain? Or just Northumberland?

There are more than just rabbits in the garden. There's something tall and shadowy moving in the trees.

It's him. He's tall — almost as tall as my cousin Tom, who plays football for the secondary school. His face is different too, older and longer. He's got muscles now and strong brown arms. But his eyes are the same.

"Molly," he says. "It's Molly, isn't it?"

He kisses his hand and blows the kiss to me. I can feel it land on my cheek and something falls onto my collar. It's a flower. A little red flower.

"Thank you," I say.

He's got something strung over his shoulder — a horn, perhaps, or a bow, or a quiver of arrows, I can't see which. Did he make it himself? There's no wind, but the trees move around him and the rabbits lift their brown heads and stare.

"The Holly King," I say. "He's still here." I'm sure he is — I'm sure he hasn't gone. Sometimes, when I'm out in the lane, I see the trees rustling in the wind, and I know it isn't me or my green god who's moving them. He hangs in the air like an unanswered question.

"Let him be," says the boy, who's almost a man. He holds out his hand to me, and then he's gone, leaving me holding the red flower and wondering if he was ever really there at all.

54

Grandma

Every Wednesday now, Emily and I go ice-skating. We're in a class with lots of other kids — mostly girls. We hang around with the others, but we're Best Friends, us two.

Emily wants to be a farmer like her dad. Or an actress, or a dancer, or maybe an ice-skater, she can't decide.

"We could run a skating shop!" says Emily. "You could sell skating boots and food from my farm and your dad's newspaper."

"We could write our own newspaper!"

"We could write a play and I could act in it," says Emily.

I've never met anyone who likes stories and make-believe as much as me, except for Mum, and she's a mum, so doesn't count. We have so much to say, we're still talking when we get home. Emily's mum talks to Grandma, and we plan everything out.

"It wouldn't matter even if our shop never sold

anything," says Emily. "That's the nice thing about farms, no one ever starves."

After Emily's gone, Grandma comes and stands in the kitchen doorway with her coffee.

"Got time enough for all that?" she says, looking at our plans.

"Course," I say.

Grandma snorts.

"We aren't doing it all this year," I explain. "Maybe some of it. But, like, it takes ages to become a good enough skater to go to the Olympics."

"Hmm." Grandma gives me a funny look. "How long have you two been here now?" she says. "Four months?"

I count. "September, October, November, December, January, February, March. Seven months!"

"Seven!" Grandma starts. "What's that dad of yours thinking?"

I squirm. "How should I know?"

"Hmm," says Grandma. "I think," she says, "it's time I talked to your father again. This has gone on long enough."

All the muscles in my shoulders tighten. I've got used to us being here now. Surely she isn't going to throw us out too? Doesn't *anyone* want us?

"What do you mean?" I say. And then, when she doesn't answer, "Grandma? What are you going to do?"

"Me?" says Grandma. "I'm going to London."

And she finishes the last of her coffee in one long gulp.

55

Kew Gardens

It's late. Hannah and I are sitting on the stairs, waiting for Dad to come.

"D'you think Grandma doesn't want us anymore?" I say.

Hannah's drawing a broken heart on the knee of her new jeans.

"Grandpa wants us," she says, half-comfortingly.

Car noises come down the lane. Someone bangs on the door. We jump up and open it.

It's Dad.

"Has something happened?" he says. "Are you all right?"

"Grandma's going to London!" I say.

Dad catches hold of my hands, but he doesn't get a chance to say anything, because Grandma's door opens and Grandma comes out, dragging a suitcase. Grandpa follows, wearing his coat and cap and carrying a big green bag.

"Mum!" says Dad.

Grandma beams. "Toby!" she says. "At last! I was wondering if you were ever going to show up."

Dad drops my hands. "Mum," he says. "What's going on?"

"We're going to London," says Grandma. "It's about time we had a holiday."

Dad looks confused. "But —" he says. "You could have asked —"

"We could," says Grandma. "And we are. We'll be back Thursday." And she comes downstairs — bump — bump — bump like Christopher Robin, dragging her suitcase behind her.

Dad just stands there staring.

"But —" he says, and I want to giggle, he looks so confused. "Are you taking the girls?"

Grandma stops. "Really, Toby," she says. "I did think I'd taught you more sense than that. Of course we aren't taking the girls. Arthur's taking me to the V&A . . . and Knightsbridge . . . and maybe Kew Gardens. I haven't been to Kew Gardens in years."

"But . . ." says Dad.

"You don't have to open the shop," says Grandma. "But if you do close, can you leave a note in the window saying we'll be back Friday? And the girls need to be in school at nine. They've got PE tomorrow, but I'm sure they'll fill you in on all the details. Come on, chicks. Say good-bye."

She hugs Hannah and then me.

"Have fun," she whispers, and lets go before I can ask her to stay.

When Grandpa hugs me, I cling to him. "You are coming back, aren't you?"

Grandpa squeezes me. "Course we are," he whispers back. "Grandma just wants your dad to spend some time with you. That's all."

I keep my arms around his neck, remembering what happened last time.

"You're coming back Thursday?"

"Thursday," says Grandpa. "Promise."

In the house, I'm sure it's going to be like that horrible weekend in Newcastle, only this time Grandpa isn't around to rescue us. Dad doesn't know what to do. He stands in the hall, his funny, ugly face screwed up helplessly.

"Do you people know what that was about?" he says eventually.

"Who cares?" says Hannah. "D'you want a cup of tea?"

She makes tea in the teapot, the way Grandpa does. I

sit as close to Dad as I can. I wonder, if I love him hard enough, if I can persuade him to stay.

"Are you staying here?"

"I'm going to have to, aren't I?" he says. "Lucky I've got so much holiday saved up." He pats my hand. Then he looks around him, probably pleased to be back in a clean kitchen again. "This is great tea, Hannah," he says.

56

Back

Next morning, it's Dad who wakes me up, wearing one of Grandpa's checked shirts and Grandma's shop apron.

"Up, up, up!" he says, banging on the back of a saucepan with a spoon.

I rub my eyes.

"It's half past *seven*," Hannah groans, from her room. "We don't have to get up yet!"

"Don't you?" says Dad. He sounds surprised. At home, we had to be up in time to drive to school. Here, it's just down the hill.

He's set the table for breakfast. He's bought me another present: Coco Pops from the shop. When I lived with Mum and Dad, I only liked Coco Pops for breakfast, but now I like Frosties and Weetabix and eggs if Grandpa is making them.

"Molly doesn't eat that anymore," says Hannah. "And I don't eat cereal either. I have toast, like Grandma."

Dad doesn't wash the breakfast things up, like Grandpa. He leaves them in the sink with last night's mugs. He clearly cares less about tidying than I remember him caring. And at ten to nine, when Hannah says, "You're supposed to tell us to go now," he looks at his watch and says, "Off you trot, then!" without asking if we've got our topic books or pencil cases or papier-mâché model of the Middlesbrough Transporter Bridge.

In the front yard, we stop and look at each other.

"Dad's back!" I say.

"Not forever," says Hannah. "But no smelly Grandma bossing us about!" And she runs off down the hill, school bag bouncing on her back.

When we get home, he's in the shop, selling stamps to Alexander's dad.

"Afternoon!" he says. "Want an egg?" And he throws us a Cadbury's Creme Egg each.

"You're happy," says Hannah. He is. He makes us proper Dad homemade bread, which doesn't rise in Grandma's oven either, but tastes just as chewy as it always did at home.

By Thursday, we're used to having him to ourselves. It's a shock to think he's going home soon.

After school, before Grandpa and Grandma get back,

I help him in the shop. I stack all the new tins and things on the shelves. I mop the floor. I sell sherbet fountains to Sascha and her little sister.

"If I was your grandma," says Dad, "I'd give you a job."

He looks so happy, I risk asking him again.

"Don't you want to stay?"

Dad puts his arm around me.

"I wish I could," he says. "But I can't take your grandma's job. I've got my own work. You know that."

I lean my head against his stomach.

"So you can't have us."

"No."

"And we're Grandma's responsibility now."

"Well." He squeezes me. "Maybe a bit mine too."

I look up. "If you had another job, would you have us back?"

He doesn't answer for the longest time. Then he says, "Would you want me?"

I nod.

"I —" He stops, but then he starts again. "I might not always get things right."

"I don't always get things right," I say. "I get things wrong, all the time I get things wrong. And you don't mind, do you?"

"Oh, Moll," says Dad. "Never. Never, ever."

"Well, then."

Dad's quiet. "There's a job coming up," he says. "Sub-editor. Working for someone I know from university. It's the other side of the city, but the hours are better. And you can cope for a few hours after school on your own, can't you?"

"Yes!" I say. "Do it!"

"It's only a maybe," says Dad. "I might not get it. You do understand that, don't you, Moll? It's nothing definite."

"You'll get it," I say. "You will, won't you?"

"I don't know," says Dad. Then he squeezes me suddenly, so I can feel my ribs pressing against my organs. "Keep it to yourself," he says. "But, yes. I think I will."

57

The Midnight Hunter

So that's Dad sorted. One down and one to go. If Grandma can sort Dad, can I sort the Holly King?

The night Dad goes, I can't sleep. I lie and listen to Grandma and Grandpa moving about downstairs. I can hear people laughing on the radio, and Grandpa singing as he rinses out the tea mugs, and Grandma doing the accounts, asking Grandpa, "Do you know why everyone seems to be buying cotton buds all of a sudden?"

If I push my head outside my curtains, I can see a deep blue dusk, with a single star hanging in the sky over the hills. I wrap my arms around Humphrey and rest my chin on his head. It's perfectly quiet. It's perfectly still. No one's out.

And then I see him.

He's standing in the shadows, watching the shop. It's him. The horned god, the Holly King. It makes me gasp, seeing him so close.

It's the same thick body, the strong, flat, animal-ish

face. But he looks older, darker. And he's standing, without the horse he had before. He looks less like a man and more like an animal, bent and hunched against the wall.

I don't know why he's here, and I don't worry now, because now my own man's here, coming up the hill from the village on a gray horse. When the Holly King sees him he turns and runs, head bent, body down, in and out of the circle of streetlamp light and down the lane.

My man stops his horse and looks up at the house. I stick my head out of the window.

"He went that way!"

My man shakes his head. He's older again. A real man now.

"Come down!" he calls. "Come down and join the hunt!"

I hesitate, just for a moment, then I pull my head out of the window and start scrabbling under my bed for my shoes.

I don't wait to get dressed. I just take my coat off the hook and pull it on over my pajamas. There's a jiggle of excitement where my heart is as I let myself out the back door. I always wanted to do this, go out alone in the middle of the night. I never understood how the Famous Five dared. But tonight, I'm not afraid. Tonight, there's a man on a tall horse. Tonight, the moon is round and silver, and tonight the air is sharp and cold and tonight the sky is a deep, deep blue and there's this one bright star shining over the hills and I'm out without anyone knowing, and I want to sing.

He's waiting beside the wall. He's not got a saddle or a bridle — he looks like he's stolen someone's horse straight out of its field. Maybe he has. He's wearing what I think is a cloak, but when I get close I see it's a deerskin. A real deerskin, with four dangly leg-skins, but no head. It's tied round his neck by the front legs and the rest hangs down his back. There's a strong, thick smell, frightening and exciting at the same time.

"Come on, then," he says, and holds out his hand.

I've only ever been on a horse once before and that was a pony, really. I'm not frightened, though. I climb on the wall and my man reaches down and lifts me up by my armpits, and there's a messy, scrabbly moment when he's pulling and I'm holding on to the horse's mane, and then suddenly it's all right and here I am, sitting up in front of him.

I look at him and I look at the house and I laugh out loud.

"Look," he says and he shows me something. It's a horn — the sort you blow and the sort that belongs to an animal, both. The narrow bit at the end is made of what looks like gold, but the long curved body comes from an animal. I don't know which sort.

"Can I?" I say, and he nods.

I put my mouth round the horn and blow, but all that comes out is a sputtery noise. My man laughs. He takes the horn off me and holds it up in one dark arm and then he blows.

This wonderful noise comes out — *Turaaahh! Turaaahh! Turaaahh!* — it's a hunt-call and a warning and a challenge, all rolled into one. The horse rears up on its hind legs and my man's arm tightens around my waist and he blows the horn again — *Turaaahh! Turaaahh!* — and we're off.

Off down the lane, the horse's hooves clattering on the road. Off, with the wind in my hair and my man's arm tight around my chest and my fingers clinging on to the horse's mane. We really are going faster than fairies, faster than witches, faster than roller coasters and sledges, faster than ice-skating or bicycles, much faster than Chloe's fat pony. We leap over a hedge and my man blows into the horn — *Turaaahh! Turaaahh!*

And I realize that we aren't alone — there are other shapes crashing through the hedges, low and dark and fierce and hot — dogs with black legs and white teeth.

There are other huntsmen around and behind us, wild huntsmen, and I look back at my man and see the shadowy outline of horns growing up out of his head, and all of a sudden, I'm afraid. I've been here before. I remember this — the night, the wild hunt and the hunted man, only this time my man isn't hunted, he's the hunter.

The huntsmen plow forward into the night. The dogs howl. My man spurs his horse onward, over and through the hedges, branches and leaves digging into my legs and tearing at my clothes. "Stop!" I shout, "*Stop!*" but he just laughs. He's different again; wilder, more dangerous. I cling to the horse's mane and squeeze my legs tight around his belly. The Oak King's arm still holds me, but he's laughing now and urging the dogs on. If I fall off, I'll be crushed under the horses' hooves and — I realize with a sudden start of fear — he won't go back for me. He won't even notice I'm gone.

I want him to stop. I want to tell him I've changed my mind, to let the Holly King go. I'm frightened. Everything is mixed up in my head — who's good, who's bad, who's right, who's wrong. I can do nothing except cling to the horse's mane and wait for it to end, however it will end.

We pour through the fields, through the night. Above us, the stars whirl. Below us, the world is turning. Winter is over. It's the spring equinox, and tonight a new rule begins.

The dogs are howling. They've seen what they're looking for. A man, running. They pour down the hill like black water and cover him. He holds one hand up over his face, but he's down, covered with dogs, and I see that he doesn't have horns anymore, he's just a man, and I'm screaming and screaming and my man has pulled in his horse and he's watching, just watching, without doing anything,

and then . . .

And then it's over.

The world is still. The hunt is gone. There's nobody here but us — me and the horned Oak King on our horse and the Holly King down on the grass, one hand still raised above his head. He's bleeding, but he's still alive. He stares at us. He doesn't speak.

I'm crying, tears rolling down my cheeks. I'm crying because I thought that the Oak King was good and the Holly King bad, but it's not that simple. Because if you want the summer, the winter must die, and if you want the winter, the summer must die too — because Persephone must go down under the green earth — because the world must turn — because the Holly King and the Oak King must fight and one must defeat the other.

My man — and he's the horned huntsman now, the leader of the wild hunt — my man stands straight on his tall horse. He doesn't say anything to the Holly King and he doesn't say anything to me. He looks down at him, lying there on the grass. Then he pulls on the horse's mane and turns it round, back toward the village, toward home.

58

Talking to Miss Shelley

At school, I'm tired. Miss Shelley is talking about suspension bridges, but her words are flowing over my head like water and I can't catch them. The bridge she's drawn on the whiteboard is stuck to the ground, so how can it be suspended?

I just blink when Alexander tries to get me to sign his petition to bring back chips in school lunches.

"It's all right for you lot," he says. "You get chips at home. My parents never give me so much as a French fry! And it's not like chips don't have vitamins. They're potatoes, aren't they? They're practically our national food. I'm being denied a valuable cultural experience!"

"We have a national food?" I say, and Alexander shakes his head and goes off after Emily.

When the bell rings for break, Miss Shelley calls me back.

"You all right, Molly?" she says.

It strikes me as funny that after all that's happened

this year — Mum dying, Dad leaving, my man dying and then coming back — she picks today to ask if I'm all right.

"Yes . . ." I say. Then, "Miss Shelley, you remember the wild hunt?"

"Yes."

"Is it good? Or bad?"

Miss Shelley tucks her hair behind her ear. She looks at me thoughtfully.

"You know," she says, "I've never been able to work that one out."

"Don't the stories say?"

"Oh, stories," she says. "I wouldn't trust stories. They can never agree with themselves from one day to the next." She rubs the back of her neck with her hand. "Spring equinox last night," she says.

"It was?"

"Oh yes." She looks at me and then, suddenly, she laughs. "Don't look so worried, Molly!" she says. "They won't be back till Beltane. And they didn't hurt you, did they?"

"They . . . You mean they're *real*?"

"I couldn't begin to comment," says Miss Shelley seriously. "All questions not relating to long division or man-made bridging structures should be directed to the questioner's pagan or religious figure of choice." The sun has brought out new freckles on her nose and for a moment she looks so much like my mum that it hurts. "Alternatively, you could go and have a look at the mess the horses made of the lane," she says. "Whichever."

59

A Game I Stopped Playing

And now summer's here. Blue sky — sometimes — and sandals and checked school dresses, and sun warm enough to leave our coats at home. There are daisies on the lawn and dandelions on the tarmac and cow parsley and foxgloves growing on the banks by the lane.

Dad gets the job in Newcastle. We're going back to live with him as soon as he's managed to sell our house, probably at the end of term, Grandpa says. He puts in an offer on a funny little terraced house at the other side of the city, with a long dandelion-y garden and a sycamore tree with a tire swing. There's a school for me at the end of the road and a rough, tough secondary school with a hockey team and a youth club and guitar lessons for Hannah.

"About time too!" says Grandma, but Grandpa busies himself with the tea things and doesn't say anything.

"Won't you miss us?" says Hannah, and Grandma snorts.

"Hopeful, aren't you?" she says. Then she sees the look on Hannah's face and softens. "Maybe a bit. We've gotten used to having you around, messing the place up."

"You'll have to come and stay, in half term," says Grandpa, and Hannah says we will.

At school, we're allowed back out onto the playing fields and we have a giant grass fight with all the cut grass. The little ones build nests in it, for Barbie and Sylvanian Families and Action Men. Sometimes Emily and I help them, though we're much too old for baby games, of course.

When we aren't playing with the littlies, we go off on our own, Alexander and Emily and me. We climb the trees at the edge of the field and tell secrets. Emily tells us how her dad is going to teach her to drive a tractor, because you don't need a driving license if you have your own field, and he'll teach us too when we go round to her house. Alexander tells us how he hates playing football, because the other boys always make him goalkeeper and he always lets the goals in.

"What's it like living with your gran?" says Alexander, and I screw up my nose.

"It's nice living in the country," I say. "But I miss my dad."

"What's it like not having a mum?" says Emily in her soft voice. I think about it.

"Lonely," I say. "Better now Dad's coming back. But still lonely."

"You've got us now," says Emily, but it isn't the same.

When we're not telling secrets, we're making plans. We're going to write a book — have a club — build a tree house. We get very excited when we think about the summer, then Emily says, "But Molly won't be here. She'll be in Newcastle."

"I'll visit," I say. But who knows when that will be?

We go back down to Newcastle for the weekend, twice. The house isn't as clean as I remember it being, but all the moldy peppers have gone. Dad takes us out to the pub to meet his friend, who owns a newspaper and lets us lose all his money on the fruit machines. We go ice-skating, and we go for a walk in the park and pick up snails and bits of wood like we used to with Mum, and we try to remember what living with each other was like.

"At the end of term," Dad says, "we'll be home together again." And I lie in bed at night in the lightness of summer evenings, watching the shadows from my leaf mobile sailing across my wall, and try to imagine having a home again.

So many things are happening that I don't have time to think about my man. He seems to have gone now, anyway. As the summer goes on, he gets further and further away, like someone I invented or a game I stopped playing. I went back to his barn once after the wild hunt, but it was empty. Half of the wall had fallen in, and no one could live there now.

60

End

But I do see him again.

It's my birthday in May. We go to Kielder Forest for the day. Dad, Grandpa, Grandma, Hannah, Emily, Alexander, and me.

It was never going to be perfect, but it's enough.

The world seems to know that it's my birthday. The sky is blue from one edge to the other, with fluffy little clouds like lambs' wool. The forest is full of birds and green leaves and dappled sunlight. My present from Auntie Meg is a new grown-up skirt with beads on it and little mirrors. It's almost exactly the same green as the trees and it makes me feel like something magical, something not exactly human.

We spread out our picnic by a stream. Hannah lies in the grass and reads her magazine, but Emily and Alexander and I go paddling. We splash Hannah and she squeals. We splash her again and she runs down to the stream and splashes us back.

Soon, Hannah's leaving primary school forever. She'll be even more grown-up than she is now. It's nice to have her join in with us for once, while we still have her.

After lunch, Grandpa and Grandma settle down under the trees and the rest of us play tag. Dad's It. He chases us all around the grass and into the edge of the forest. We go up as close to him as we dare, teasing him, and then run away again before he can catch us.

Dad's chasing me, but I run and he gets Emily instead. Emily gets Hannah and Hannah gets Alexander and Alexander comes after me.

I'm bubbling up with happiness. It's my birthday and no one can catch me. I run straight into the forest, then round again to confuse Alexander. The light is dappled and mysterious and the air is full of a green, living smell, of leaves and moss and tree bark. I can feel the earth sinking under my sandals and the breeze against my skirt. Behind me, Alexander has given up and is chasing Emily, but I carry on running.

Somewhere in front of me is movement. Feet running, or dancing. Trees rustling. I burst forward into the clearing, and suddenly I'm part of the dance.

It's like it was in the storm, when the trees held me,

but this time they are dancing. I can feel the joy shivering through them. I am lifted and spun and passed to other arms, which lift me and spin me again. Shapes move — shadowy, laughing dancers, almost human.

I'm placed down on the ground again. I land awkwardly, and almost fall. Hands reach out and take mine, strong and warm. I look up, into the eyes that I know go with the hands.

His hair is thick and brown and curly. His trousers are a greeny brown, like the trees. A wreath of leaves and yellow flowers falls over one ear. His face is laughing but his eyes are the same as they always are, deep and brown and kind.

He takes my hand and leads me to the center of the clearing. He dances me, very slowly and carefully. Around us the trees bow and sway. The air is full of the smell of flowers and leaves. Even the sunlight seems to be dancing.

He bows to me, once, not dropping his eyes, and lets go of my hand. I know what's going to happen, and I watch for as long as I can, but he whirls around and is gone.

I am left there breathless, green leaves in my hair, sunlight swirling around me, alone.

Behind me in the trees, Emily and Alexander and

Hannah are calling. Mingled with them is Dad's voice, deep and familiar and full of laughter.

I stand for a long moment there in the clearing, one arm still out before me.

Then I turn and run back into the game.

Acknowledgments

Thanks go to Nicola Bowerman, who first gave me the Oak King myth, and to Christina Oakley Harrington of Treadwell's Books for reminding me that every story is told and retold, and showing me some of the places people have taken this one. Thanks to Tara Button for all those afternoons writing in coffee shops and to Tom Harris for being understanding about the need to take a laptop on holiday and other writing-related traumas. Also for repeated computer-fixing and general loveliness.

Many thanks to everyone real and virtual who listened to me burble and complain, who told their friends about my books or who read versions of this one in production. Thanks to my editor, Marion Lloyd, for saying nice things about the manuscript and then pointing out all the ways it could be improved. Thanks to Caro Humphries, Phil Hoggart, and Emma Wiseman for letting me play Cinderella and pay rent by cooking them lentil moosh. And thank you to everyone at Scholastic for coming over all Fairy Godmother-ish, and changing everything.

This book was designed by Elizabeth B. Parisi and Kristina Iulo.

The text was set in Adobe Caslon Pro,

designed by Carol Twombly, based on the type designs of William Caslon.

The display text was set in Wordy Diva, designed by The Chank Company.

The book was printed and bound

at R. R. Donnelley in Crawfordsville, Indiana.

Production was supervised by Cheryl Weisman,

and manufacturing was supervised by Adam Cruz.